The Concrete

by

Mike Deavin

ISBN: 978-1-291-59641-0

Copyright © 2013 Mike Deavin

All rights reserved, including the right to reproduce this book, or portions thereof in any form. No part of this text may be reproduced, transmitted, downloaded, decompiled, reverse engineered, or stored, in any form or introduced into any information storage and retrieval system, in any form or by any means, whether electronic or mechanical without the express written permission of the author.

This is a work of fiction. Names and characters are the product of the author's imagination and any resemblance to actual persons, living or dead, is entirely coincidental.

PublishNation, London
www.publishnation.co.uk

To

Janet, Emma and Ben

The Concrete Grave

Chapter One

How could she do it?

This was the overriding thought that consumed Andy as he left his nineteen-sixties built, semi-detached house in Crampton, a small village in Hampshire.

As he got into his car and started the engine, he checked the clock. Five thirty in the morning, his usual time. He reversed out of the short drive and headed for the local station, Petersfield, about twelve minutes drive away.

It was a damp, miserable Tuesday morning in November and the tarmac road still glistened from the overnight rain. The local radio station droned on in the background but Andy paid no attention. He had other things on his mind this morning.

The roads were quiet, one of the few advantages of leaving home at an unearthly hour. Andy parked in his usual side road next to a monstrous new DIY warehouse. Parking was unrestricted here and free; the station charged eight pounds for the day, no way was Andy going to pay that - his meagre salary couldn't afford almost two thousand pounds a year just to park his car.

Why did she do it?

Andy considered this as he walked towards the station whilst fumbling for his season ticket; the time was five forty-five, giving him just enough time to catch the five fifty train to Waterloo, his usual train. He had to be on site before eight o'clock or the whole day would be chaos. Andy was the project manager, and without him things just wouldn't happen as they should.

How could I let her do it?

Andy stood on platform one at Petersfield station and pushed his uncombed, curly ginger hair away from his eyes. The time was five forty-nine; he had arrived, as usual, one minute early. He looked around his dark, damp surroundings, remarkably busy considering the time of day, as commuters stood in their usual positions reading newspapers or checking their smartphones for e-mails, which were starting to land in their already overcrowded inboxes.

The train arrived, mercifully on time, and Andy took his usual window seat. At least the early hour meant he always got a seat. By the time the train arrived at Woking there was standing room only. A colleague once told him that train journeys gave you the gift of time and Andy would normally use that gift to reflect on the day ahead and browse his copy of *The Metro*, the free newspaper which he grabbed as he went through the ticket barrier. Today was different; all he could think of were the events of the previous evening.

Andy had known Jane for almost a year. He had met her, in the unlikeliest of circumstances, at Waterloo station. He was dashing, as usual, through the automated ticket barriers onto the main concourse. He pushed his ticket through the barrier and rushed forward. Andy always rushed. He also neglected to take his season ticket, which had cost him close to twelve hundred pounds for three months. He walked on only to be accosted a few seconds later by an attractive, but out of breath, young lady, so out of breath, in fact, that she could hardly speak.

"Excuse me, I think this is yours," she said, holding out a slightly screwed up train ticket in her right hand.

Andy looked first at the ticket, then at her. Without really thinking Andy said, "I don't think so, I have mine here," taking his wallet out and opening it. "Oh, it's not there. Wow, thanks very much, how did you get it?"

"You left it at the barrier after you'd pushed it through," she said, regaining her breath and passing him his ticket.

Her bright red coat, the sweet smile, the shoulder-length blonde hair which fell across part of her face and the fragrance of her perfume all combined to trigger a reaction which surprised even Andy. She was average height and despite her coat it was clear she had a well-formed figure. She had an air of confidence about every move she made. She was stunning and Andy couldn't believe his luck.

"Can I buy you a coffee or something?" he said, regardless of the fact that he had to be on site before eight o'clock and it was now nearly seven thirty. The reaction was uncharacteristic; spontaneity never had been Andy's strongest attribute.

"Sorry, I don't have time, and by the looks of it you don't either," she said with a smile. She gracefully hooked her hair back behind her right ear and it helped to frame her face. She then turned smartly on one foot and walked away.

Andy was mesmerised by the whole experience and stood, open-mouthed, watching her walk briskly away. He rapidly gathered himself and continued walking towards the Jubilee Line as the mystery lady disappeared down the escalator towards the other three underground lines that ran through Waterloo. Andy headed on to work and couldn't help thinking that he had missed a golden opportunity.

His day was busy and he hadn't had much time to think of the incident until that same evening when he was walking back across the concourse at Waterloo. Unbelievably he saw that bright red coat going through the barrier at platform nine, his platform. He ran towards her, zigzagging around the passengers walking across his path, pushed his ticket through the barrier and eventually caught up with her just as she was stepping into her chosen carriage.

"Hi, I remembered it this time," shouted Andy, holding his ticket proudly at arm's length. On this occasion it was his turn to be breathless.

"Well done," she replied sarcastically, "one out of two isn't bad." She quickly followed it with that smile that had so beguiled Andy only a few hours earlier, moved into the carriage and sat down on an empty double seat.

"Do you mind?" said Andy.

"Not at all," she replied.

"Andy," he said, courteously holding out his hand.

"Jane," she replied, quickly returning the handshake.

They discovered quickly that they had a lot in common; they lived in the same village and had similar interests. The journey flew by. They both alighted at Petersfield and Andy turned the earlier coffee invitation into one for a drink at the local pub. Jane said yes and the rest is, as they say, history.

The Concrete Grave

Jane had seemed so easy to talk to. He told her about the messy divorce he was going through and Jane had listened intently. Things blossomed quickly and they moved in together six months later. For three months he was as happy as he had been for ages and it felt as though he had known Jane for many years. However, recently things had got a little strained and Andy had no idea why. Until last night. He looked through the train window at the blackness beyond and continued reflecting on the events of the previous evening.

*

Andy arrived home late, a little after nine thirty; he had had problems with a concrete pump breaking down and the one hundred square metres of concrete slab which was being poured had taken three hours longer than it should have done. Temporary floodlights were needed so that the job could be finished. Andy wouldn't normally have noticed his credit card bill; he didn't bother about such things and recently Jane had taken responsibility for all of their financial matters. But on this occasion the bill hadn't been put back into the envelope properly and the total owed was screaming at him from the kitchen worktop; eleven thousand, eight hundred and fifty-three pounds, twenty-nine pence. Surely he had misread it. The paper was at an angle and a figure that large was simply unbelievable. Andy turned the bill around and pulled it out of the envelope.

The Concrete Grave

"What are you looking at?" Jane exclaimed as she snatched the bill and envelope from Andy's hand.

"What am I looking at? What am I looking at?" Andy repeated, trying to keep as calm as possible, struggling to keep his anger in check. "That is a very good question, my credit card bill - that's what I am looking at."

"It is nothing for you to worry about," said Jane, trying to calm down quickly. "And what's your excuse for being late tonight? Your fancy French architect stayed late on site again did she?" Jane always thought the best form of defence was attack, and attack she did.

"What are you talking about? No she didn't. And if you must know we had a concrete pump break down and I had to stay to the end of the slab pour." His head was spinning as he looked at the credit card bill screwed up in Jane's hand. "And don't change the subject, we need to talk about this credit card bill. There is clearly an error and we need to sort it before we start getting charged interest."

Andy walked from the kitchen to the lounge and sat on the settee; the remote control for the television was on the coffee table and Liverpool were live on Sky. Turning the match on now would not be the best idea.

"What's for supper?"

"Well, it was a pasta bake, but as it has been in the oven for the past two hours it probably isn't any more," Jane replied.

"That'll be fine," he said, hoping to calm Jane's mood and she gave it to him on a lap tray complete with fork and a slice of crusty brown bread.

The Concrete Grave

"These credit card companies," moaned Andy as he stuffed the dry brown substance from the plate in front of him into his mouth, "are absolutely useless, just how can they make a mistake like that?"

Andy looked at Jane who had sat in the armchair to his left. She had suddenly gone quiet, very quiet, and her pretty blue eyes filled with tears which started running down both cheeks. Andy realised that this was the first time he had seen Jane cry. She was usually very robust, never wanting to display any sign of weakness. She was five years younger than him, but always seemed very together in all aspects of her life. She had left school after she had taken her GCSE's and got a job with the government. Andy was not quite sure what she did, but she seemed to work long, irregular hours.

He reached for the box of tissues on the coffee table, being careful not to tip the remains of his meal on the floor, and gently passed her a tissue.

"Don't worry, we'll sort it out. I'll give Mumbai a call tomorrow and I'm sure Kevin from Rangoon will correct the mistake," Andy said, trying to lighten the mood.

The look on Jane's face frightened him, she always smiled at his little jokes, but this evening her face was swollen from the tears which had continued to fall.

"Kevin won't be able to help us this time, Andy," she said. "I've got us into a bit of a mess."

"This train is approaching its final destination; please remember to take all your personal belongings with you."

The Concrete Grave

The unnecessarily loud public address system on the train shook him out of his thoughts. It was just after seven o'clock - where had the last seventy five minutes gone?

Andy gathered up his untouched copy of *The Metro*, grabbed his rucksack and made for the ticket barriers. He crossed the forecourt towards the Jubilee Line underground station still worrying about last night's argument.

The eastbound platform was as crowded as usual. He stood dutifully in line for his usual door and waited zombielike with his fellow commuters.

The tube was packed. Only as it left Canary Wharf was he able to get a seat. He unfolded his copy of *The Metro* for the first time and turned to the back page. Wayne Rooney in trouble again. No change there then, he thought.

He alighted at Canning Town station, a modern station in a part of London which time seemed to have forgotten. He proceeded to the exit. He still had a twelve-minute walk before he reached his construction site.

He turned and walked alongside the very busy A13 main road and over the renowned Canning Town flyover as it rose over the quaintly, but inappropriately, named Bow Creek. Way below him was a rubbish recycling plant that in the dawn light was slowly coming to life; already men were hand picking through bins of rubbish. I wouldn't want that job for all the tea in China, Andy thought - doubting that the operatives were even earning the minimum wage.

The cold damp air hit him as he turned west and he buttoned up his coat rapidly. To the south the white dome of the O2 looked like a giant mammal rising out of a mist-covered sea, as the breaking dawn created a phosphory luminescence across the East London skyline.

The London Borough of Tower Hamlets was the most varied of all the London boroughs; it had the poorest areas of London in its famous East End as well as some of the wealthiest. Canary Wharf was the famous centrepiece of the redeveloped Docklands area; Andy could just see the outline of the cloud shrouded tower as he strode towards his destination.

He turned right into Clay Street, passing rows of houses in various states of disrepair, and he felt about as flat as the gasometer behind the three-storey terrace houses of Norman Road. The three fifteen-storey tower blocks in the distance – a crime wave in themselves – poked their ugly heads into the skyline. The tone of the neighbourhood was set by the full-height steel shutters which covered the doors and windows of all the shops along a short parade. One of the fast food establishments was called *Prestige Fried*. Andy doubted that the quality of the fare on sale matched the name.

He turned the final corner, and ahead of him was St. Oswald's Primary School with the temporary site offices stacked neatly to one side.

St. Oswald's was Andy Walker's second school construction project in Tower Hamlets; he'd been making the two hour fifteen minute commute for almost two years. The construction industry had been hit hardest by the recession. Beggars couldn't be choosers. He needed the work and the salary that went with it, and after what happened last night he really did need the money.

The Concrete Grave

He entered the pedestrian site gate and had just started to climb the outside stairs to his first-floor Portacabin, when he was accosted by Sean, the groundworks foreman. Sean was a typical Irish tradesman, skilled at what he did and very hard-working. His untidy mop of hair suited his rugged complexion. His ruddy cheeks suggested that his fondness for Guinness was not restricted to the recommended daily alcohol intake.

Andy liked Sean. They had worked together before, and the feeling was mutual, but Andy could see that Sean was not in the best of moods this morning.

"Do you know what those thieving bastards have done?" he yelled.

"No, I don't," said Andy, "I have just walked through the gate after a tiring journey and all I want is a cup of coffee."

"Six batteries – all six batteries!" Sean cursed.

"What six batteries? What are you talking about?" said Andy. By this time he was nearing the top of the stairs, the sanctuary of his office and the beckoning kettle.

Sean followed Andy into the office and filled the kettle in the adjacent kitchen, realising that it was pointless relating anything to him until he'd had his first morning dose of caffeine.

The site set up was typical of any you would find around the country. Four portable office units, ten metres long and three metres wide stacked in two pairs. The canteen and toilets were at ground level with the offices and meeting room on the first floor. An external staircase ran between the two

The Concrete Grave

blocks. Andy's office could best be described as functional; six metres long, with white walls and a pale vinyl-covered floor. Two back-to-back desks were in the centre, with a solitary filing cabinet at one side next to a large rack where dozens of site drawings were hanging down from clips. There was a large flat worktop under the end window where the drawings could be laid out. The walls were populated with the odd drawing showing the final elevations of the school and a marked-up construction programme, which showed the project further behind programme than it should be. The only bright spot around the entire perimeter wall was the spot where a tasteful Kylie Minogue calendar hung, to the left of which Andy was busily setting up his laptop. The office had an unmistakeable smell of bleach; the cleaners had clearly been over-enthusiastic again last night.

"Now, that's more like it," Andy said as he took his first gulp, "Thanks, Sean. Now what's this about six batteries?"

"Stolen. Someone has broken into site, removed each and every battery from our four machines. That means no work will get done today and, as we are paid for the work we do, it means none of us will get a penny."

"The little sods," said Andy, "I'll call the police."

"And just what do you expect them to do about it?" Sean said.

"Probably nothing, but I need a crime number for the paperwork."

Andy had known that the site was particularly vulnerable from the start. It was surrounded by high rise tenement style buildings, constructed in the nineteen-sixties and inhabited by largely unemployed residents, who seemed to spend most of their spare time standing on the open balcony watching the progress on site. Presumably they were biding their time for their first 'hit', which he had now discovered was probably last night.

Andy had urged Steve Biggins, a construction director and his line manager, to install a resident night-time security guard from day one as it was obvious they would have problems. But times were hard. To win this job costs had to be cut and costly security was one of the first things to go.

"Sean?" Andy said thinking. "Tell me, exactly what on earth will these crooks do with six large industrial batteries from random dumpers and diggers?"

"Flog 'em," Sean said. "Probably get about twenty quid each – they'll cost us closer to two hundred to replace."

"I'm not worried about the cost - it's the lack of production that concerns me. We are already two weeks behind programme and we are only in week ten. Not a good start."

"I'll ring the yard and see if they have any spares, if not we'll have to order them and wait," groaned Sean.

The office door suddenly burst open.

"Have you heard, Andy? The little buggers they've..."

"Yes, Dave, I know, six batteries have gone and with them at least one day's production."

Dave Baron was Andy's assistant, a 'salt of the earth' site man who was in his late fifties and had worked his way up to the position after starting life as a bricklayer. Dave believed that computers, e-mails and websites were for wimps - for him a project was built on site, no point wasting time sitting behind a laptop waiting for the next e-mail to arrive. He had to be where the action was, on site, and it was for that reason Andy liked him so much. And it was for that reason he had insisted that Dave was his number two on this project, as he had been on his previous three. His grey hair and unshaven face belied his attention to detail in the work that he did on site.

"Oh, you know. Not good news is it? We might as well put a large sign on the hoarding saying '*Help Yourself*', what with us having no security at night," said Dave, thrusting his hands into the pocket of the black logoed fleece he was wearing.

"Yes, I know, I'll speak to Steve. Maybe now he'll release some of our precious margin to pay for it. Otherwise it'll end up costing us a fortune," said Andy. "This is all I need at the start of today."

Chapter Two

Andy left the site office just after six o'clock that evening. He was usually the last to leave as he had to lock up, not an ideal situation when you're faced with a two-hour-plus journey home.

He made his way through the narrow side streets towards Canning Town tube station. It was dark and cold but at least it wasn't raining.

Andy Walker was thirty-two and had worked in the construction industry since the age of seventeen. His father had owned a plant hire company in Essex, earthmoving machinery and lorries, and one of Andy's earliest memories was sitting on the lap of the driver of a Caterpillar D8, a thirty-five ton bulldozer capable of shifting one thousand cubic metres of earth in just one hour. From that moment Andy only ever wanted to work in construction. The only toys he ever wanted centred around construction with Lego, Meccano or Airfix kits, it didn't matter which - Andy just liked putting things together.

After his moderate performance with his O Level exams Andy left school and joined Wakefield's, a national construction company based in West London as a management trainee. As a trainee, the plan was for him to spend time in all the departments within the business, from estimating to quantity surveying, as well as gaining experience on site. Andy only wanted to be on site, and he showed an aptitude for working with the labour force, so senior managers were happy to keep him in that role. He never experienced the comforts of working at head office nor did he want to.

Andy was a striking man, over six foot tall, solid but not overweight, with ginger hair. He was one of those people who always seemed to have a smile on his face and he was an eternal optimist.

At the age of twenty-five he followed Steve Biggins, who was, at that time, a contracts manager to a smaller, but more local, contractor, Chapple Construction. He was promoted to the more senior position of project manager and was given his first project, a small warehouse extension in Surrey, where he quickly established himself as one to watch for the future. But, seven years later, due to a variety of circumstances, Andy was still a project manager, albeit responsible now for larger and more complex projects.

For the first time since his early morning journey to work, his mind went back to last night. Andy had had such a difficult day, what with one problem after another, that he hadn't had time to think about anything else. Arranging for the replacement batteries was one thing but then the head of the school had phoned to complain about some of the site workers who were apparently smoking in the street, in front of the school's main reception. It had taken the best part of an hour to find out that the culprits were from the Electricity Board and had nothing to do with Andy's site. The District Surveyor had made a speculative visit in the afternoon and had condemned half of the drainage. It had been the day from hell, but then he'd had quite a few of those recently.

The Concrete Grave

Andy reached Waterloo and caught the six forty-five train. He got a seat and reflected upon what he was going to say to Jane when he got home.

During the previous night's discussion, which went on well past midnight, it had transpired that Jane had ventured on to some online gambling sites in an effort to make some quick money. Within two months she had run up debts of more than ten thousand pounds. All on Andy's credit card. Andy remembered that back in September Jane's own credit card had kept being refused. Apparently 'the chip had become worn' and she was in the process of getting a replacement when Andy, foolishly now as it turned out, gave Jane his card details and pin number. He trusted her completely and couldn't get over the shock of what she had done. Jane had promised to work overtime, or get a bank loan to pay Andy back, but it would still take a long time to clear the debt - meantime interest was building up rapidly on his credit card bill.

Andy drove up to the front of the house and parked the car. No lights were on and it was clear that Jane wasn't back yet - and just as he was getting concerned he received a text. He took out his mobile phone and he read it quickly. It was from Jane:

Sorry Andy. Working

late again don't wait up xx

In a way, Andy was relieved. Although it meant he'd have to cook for himself, it also meant that he wouldn't have to confront Jane and discuss the mess they were in. Andy didn't feel like cooking much, so he grabbed a beer from the fridge, put some baked beans in the microwave and had them on toast. He went into the lounge. The lounge was a small, neat room with a red, two-person settee and a matching armchair. A small coffee table was in the centre with an unread copy of the *Daily Express* folded neatly in the centre of it. Andy turned on the television and watched a poor game of football without taking much interest. An early night was what he really needed, and within an hour Andy was in bed and asleep.

*

He was awoken by the five o'clock alarm and was pleased to see that Jane was fast asleep beside him. He had no idea what time she got in so he was careful not to wake her as he quietly got dressed and crept down the stairs. The on-going discussions would have to wait until the evening.

Andy arrived on site at his usual time and was relieved to hear the sounds of the excavators working; obviously the stolen batteries had been replaced as planned. Dave had agreed to be on site by seven o'clock to let the plant fitter in to fit the new batteries.

It was Wednesday, and that meant a meeting. This week it was a design meeting, with the full team present to review the progress that the architect was making. Andy sat in the cramped meeting room and listened to the discussions going on around him. He was bored by the list of excuses being proffered as to why essential design information hadn't been produced.

The Concrete Grave

"Sylvie, please tell me, what *exactly* have you done during the past seven days?" Andy said sarcastically. Sylvie was the young, inexperienced architect who had responsibility for coordinating all the design for the project. She was French and, as Jane had frequently reminded Andy, she was both attractive and stylishly dressed in the French way.

"We have produced most of the door details including the ironmongery schedules," said Sylvie defiantly.

"Door details?" Andy repeated, "Door details? We don't need those for six weeks at least. We agreed at last week's meeting that you would have completed all the curtain walling and window details by now. We needed them a fortnight ago, and we must place the order with the sub-contractor by this Friday or we will face further delays."

"That certainly wasn't my understanding. Where in the minutes of last week's meeting does it say that?" said Sylvie, her face breaking into a charming smile.

Andy knew that she had him. He had been so busy he hadn't written up the minutes; he had some scribbled notes in his daybook but that could hardly be used as compelling evidence.

"When can we have the curtain walling details then?" Andy said in a resigned tone.

"Next week, no problem," replied Sylvie.

Andy looked around at the faces of the others at the meeting. The structural engineer faintly shook his head while the quantity surveyor merely closed his eyes. It had been the same response at the last four meetings; essential design information would always be ready 'next week'.

Andy had had enough. He stood up, picking up his book and pen and left the meeting room.

"Same time next week then guys," he said as he closed the door loudly behind him.

*

"What a bunch of wasters," muttered Andy as he sipped his mug of coffee some twenty minutes later.

"Who?" Dave said, only part listening to what Andy was saying.

"That architects practice - where did the Technical Department find them? Yellow Pages I guess. They haven't got a clue how to design a school. I wouldn't let them design a brick shithouse."

"Cheap."

"What?"

"Cheap. They were probably a lot cheaper than anyone else, so they got the job. Simple, that's the way things work nowadays," said Dave perceptively.

"And no doubt they save money by using twenty-five-year-old, postgraduate architects who haven't got a clue," said Andy.

"Correct, the older, more experienced architects have all been retired or put out to grass because they are too expensive in today's market. All architect practices are employing much younger, cheaper designers to remain competitive. It's the only way they can make a profit."

"Well, that's totally unacceptable. I've just about had enough…"

Andy's rant was cut short by the ringtone on his mobile phone; 'private number' came up on the screen.

"Andy Walker speaking."

"Andy, this is Eddie."

"Before you ask, no, I don't need any more labour at the moment." Eddie McNerney had been supplying the site with casual labour. Andy didn't really like Eddie, but his labour was cheap and hardworking.

"I wasn't ringing about that. My sources tell me that you are in a bit of a - what shall we call it? A financial predicament?"

"What? Who told you?" Andy said.

"Don't worry who, just consider me the answer to your prayers, sunshine." His strong East End accent was unmistakable.

"I can't talk now - I'm busy."

"Meet me in the Prince of Wales at six tonight, public bar," said Eddie and immediately rung off.

Andy took his phone from his ear and stared at it.

"Who was that?" Dave said.

"No one," said Andy.

"It must have been someone - you were talking to him."

"A personal matter," said Andy as he wondered how Eddie had known of his problems so soon after he had discovered them himself.

The Concrete Grave

"Those bloody bricklayers are useless," said Dave.

"Cheap," said Andy, as he put his safety helmet and gloves on to walk around site. Andy walked down the stairs from his office, turned left and entered the site. He always prided himself with running a safe, tidy and efficient construction site and Saint Oswald's was no different. The strip foundations stretched out in front of him. Work was proceeding on the excavation of the lift pit, which was usually the deepest structural element of a project of this nature. The area was clean and clear except for a small area at the top of the site where the bricklayers had recently started working. It looked like a bomb had gone off and Andy stomped in the direction of the foreman bricklayer. His first three courses of bricks from the foundations looked as though they had been laid by a seven-year-old.

"What the hell do you call that?" Andy shouted, pointing in the general direction of the laid bricks, his arm swinging in an arc covering the associated mess.

"We only started today, what do you expect?" replied the unabashed foreman.

"I'm not talking about quantity, I'm talking about quality." Andy pointed in the general direction of the site entrance. "There's the gate - use it." At the same time he used the underside of his right boot to flatten the low wall that had been constructed that day.

"I'll ring your governor and ensure that tomorrow I have tradesmen on this project."

Andy immediately turned and headed back to the office, thinking more of the phone call from Eddie than the problem with the bricklayers that his less-than-competent Procurement Department had appointed.

As the skies darkened and workers packed up to leave, Andy thought about the prospect of meeting Eddie. How could he possibly help? But at the same time, what did he have to lose? By the time six o'clock came round Andy had decided to drop into the Prince of Wales on the way home.

*

The Prince of Wales was no more than twenty metres from the site entrance - you could clearly see the decaying façade of the pub from the site-office windows and it was not the kind of establishment you would normally enter alone. In its Victorian heyday it was probably the grandest building in the neighbourhood, the centre of the community, but not today; and the competition is not great.

Andy entered the bar with caution and was surprised to see how very Victorian the interior was. There were large mirrors behind the long, mahogany bar which was topped with marble and a row of splendid porcelain-handled beer pumps. What didn't surprise him was the stained, threadbare carpet and an overpowering smell of stale beer and cigarette smoke, despite a smoking ban having been in force for the past six years.

The bar was dark and as Andy was wondering how he was going to identify Eddie, as he'd only ever spoken to him on the phone, he realised that there was only one other patron, a solid-looking, bald-headed man with heavily-tattooed forearms. Just as Andy was hoping that this man wasn't Eddie, he stood up, got out of his seat and approached him with a speed that belied his bulk.

"Andy," he said, holding out his hand, which Andy instinctively shook. "Eddie." His hand felt as if it had been clamped between two large concrete paving slabs.

"What yer having?" he said.

"Pint of lager please."

"Lager please, Sharon, and the same again for me."

The barmaid pulled the pint and poured a large Bushmills which Eddie downed in a single swallow. He put the glass down and she refilled it. Eddie passed Andy the full pint glass and turned towards a corner booth at the opposite end of the bar from where he was sitting when Andy entered. The reason for the location change quickly became apparent to Andy. The wooden booth was very discreet and, if Eddie had been there when Andy had entered, he doubted if he would have seen him.

Andy removed his rucksack and placed it on the seat beside him. He sat uneasily opposite Eddie whose wide grin displayed at least three gold teeth and it would have been obvious to anyone that Eddie was not the kind of man you would want to upset.

"What's this about?" Andy said, sounding braver than he felt.

"This is about a business proposition," said Eddie.

"What exactly is your business, Eddie? Other than hiring labour of course." Andy said, realising as soon as he had finished the question that he really didn't want to hear the answer.

"Let's just say I am a manager, just like you. A facilitator, a solver of problems."

Andy decided not to follow this with the obvious supplementary question as he had a strong feeling that he was going to get the answer anyway.

"And what exactly can I do for you?" Andy said taking his first sip from the pint he held nervously in both hands, to ensure that his shaking was not too obvious.

"A very good question, Andy, but it is probably more about what I can do for you," said Eddie, with his annoying grin getting wider, this time revealing four gold teeth.

"Okay, what can you do for me?"

"Solve your problems in a flash."

"What problems are they?"

"Come on, Andy, let's not play games. Let's just say that they relate to the difficult monetary position that you find yourself in."

"I don't know what you're talking about," said Andy, feeling more and more uneasy as the conversation progressed.

"Oh, I think you do. Would the mention of a ten grand credit card bill help refresh your memory?"

"How did you…" Andy stopped himself but realised it was too late. "Okay, so I have some money problems; lots of people do."

"Not a ten grand one they don't. Not on the sort of wages you're on."

"In the phone call you said you were the answer to my prayers - how could that be?" Andy said, wondering why he was continuing with this conversation.

"Well, the answer to that is simple, I need a little assistance with something and, for your cooperation, you will be paid ten grand - cash, no questions asked," said Eddie, the inane grin gone and now replaced by a sterner more worrying scowl.

"Is it illegal?" Andy said, before realising what a stupid question that was - sitting in a rundown pub in East London opposite someone who looked like an extra from an episode of *Prison Break*.

"It'll be a transaction, Andy. Nothing more, nothing less," said Eddie.

Andy thought quickly. He had two options; option one was to react offended and walk out, option two was to explore further. He knew that the former was not an option.

"Okay," Andy said, placing his large hands around his pint glass. "Assuming I was to accept, what would you want me to do?"

"Good, I knew we could work together. I have a package, a small package that I need to dispose of. Permanently."

"Why do you need me to assist with that?"

"Well, Andy, in this day and age not much is permanent. My package must not be found. Ever. You understand?"

"Well, yes, I think so, but I still don't get where I come into this."

"You run that building site over there," Eddie pointed in the general direction of St. Oswald's, Andy for the first time noticing the letters E-T-A-H tattooed upside down on the back of each of Eddie's fingers. Andy didn't need to be a champion on Countdown to work out what the letters spelt. He swallowed hard.

"Now, I don't have a degree in construction but on that site I suspect you have deep excavations that have to be filled with concrete. Is that correct?"

"Yes."

"Well, all I want to do is place my package in one of your deep holes just before you fill it with concrete. What could be simpler than that?"

Lots of things, thought Andy, but he was wise enough not to say it.

"What sort of package is it?"

"Too much information at this stage wouldn't be a good thing. It's a small package and I'm sure it'll be easily accommodated within the foundations of your building."

"And what exactly do you want me to do?"

"Be available one night to unlock the site gates, provide access, look the other way, then lock the gates after we've finished. Simple." Andy didn't like the way Eddie kept using the word 'simple'.

"Five grand now, and five grand upon completion."

"Now?" Andy said, alarmed at the speed these negotiations seemed to be going.

"Yes, now," said Eddie, sliding a half-inch thick, plain manila envelope across the table. "Now put that in your little rucksack quickly and I'll contact you when we're ready."

Eddie then stood up and left the pub, seemingly all in one movement, leaving Andy sitting at the table staring down at a half-full glass of lager. The fingers of both his hands were placed nervously on top of an envelope containing supposedly five thousand pounds cash. He sat there for fully five minutes before he placed the package into his rucksack and left the pub less than fifteen minutes after he had entered it.

Chapter Three

Andy sat on the tube train, his rucksack positioned between his legs. He carefully held on to the small handle on the top, aware that he had a considerable sum of money close by. Or did he? He hadn't even checked. The whole thing could have been an elaborate hoax - one of those things where there are hidden cameras and someone jumps out and says, 'Surprise, surprise'. Andy wondered what else could be in that envelope. He concluded that it was probably cut out pieces of newspaper and the whole event was a prank. Nonetheless, he was very careful to keep his rucksack held in front of him as he made his way up the escalator to Waterloo station. He got his usual train, or at least one of his usual trains. He managed to get a seat just as his text alert sounded. He took his phone from his pocket, it was from Jane:

> Home about 8, looking
>
> forward to catching up. J xx

Andy read the text and realised that because of the pressure of his job and his meeting with Eddie, he had hardly given Jane a moment's thought. He suddenly felt guilty and realised he would also arrive home not long after eight o'clock. His mind went back to that night, was it really only forty eight hours ago?

"A gambling debt - how on the earth have you managed to accrue such a huge gambling debt? Especially when you don't even gamble. Do you?" Andy had asked.

"Well, I do, Andy, I have done for a while," said Jane, tissue still in hand but her demeanour suddenly a lot calmer.

The Concrete Grave

"What happened? How?" Andy simply didn't know what to say.

"Chris, a friend of mine at work was in debt and he went onto one of these gambling sites - played roulette. He started with just fifty pounds and three hours later had won over two thousand. Easy pickings, he said. Showed me the websites and I thought I'd do the same. Get some money for a holiday." Andy was about to interject but thought better of it, and allowed Jane to continue. "I came home one evening a few weeks ago. You were working late, so I thought I'd have a go. I opened an account; it really is very easy you know, fifty pounds just like Chris. An hour later, Andy, I had four hundred and twenty pounds in my account, so I kept going. I started losing and decided to put another two hundred and fifty pounds into the account."

"From my credit card," said Andy, stating the obvious.

"Yes, I'm sorry. It was so easy at the start, if Chris could make two grand then so could I. I kept going and without realising it, I was over one thousand pounds down within an hour."

"Why didn't you just stop?"

"At the time I was really enjoying it, got a real buzz every time I won."

"Which wasn't very often by the sound of it?" Andy replied sarcastically.

"I thought the only way of rectifying the situation was to keep going," said Jane.

"There are three different accounts on this bill."

"Four," corrected Jane.

"Why? How?"

"Well, after a while a notice came up at around two thousand pounds to refuse me further credit. So I went on another site and started again. This wasn't just one evening; it happened over a number of nights and weekends, when you were working. I was enjoying it, and always thought I'd come out on top."

"Like Chris," added Andy.

"Yes, like Chris. I thought it would give us some money to do something together that we'd both enjoy."

"But why didn't you tell me?"

"How could I? By the time I realised it, I was in big trouble. I'm glad you found out. The pressure was killing me."

"Let's go to bed. It's late and we're not going to solve this now. We need to think about what we can do."

"I'll work the overtime," Jane reasoned. "I've already worked it out. I got us into this mess so I'll get us out of it."

"No, we're in this together. Let's sleep on it. Something will come up." Little did Andy know at that time just how quickly it would.

As his train pulled into Petersfield station Andy got up from his window seat trying not to disturb the snoring, overweight man in the seat next to him. It looked as though a solution had come from an unlikely source, but first Andy needed to look inside that manila envelope.

As he pulled into the drive he saw the lights in the house were on. Jane was just drawing the curtains to the lounge window; she must have got home just before him. He wondered what mood he would find her in. He was walking up the short path and, before he could get the key into the lock, the door was opened for him and Jane with a broad smile threw her arms around him and gave him a big kiss.

"Hi, Andy," she said cheerily, "How's your day been?"

Andy was taken aback, but he was also pleased. Certainly she was much happier than when he had last seen her.

"Oh, not bad I guess, but my life would be much easier if there was at least a half-competent architect in the world," he said.

"Come in, sit down, I'll get you a beer. I collected a takeaway on the way home, Chinese. Are you ready for it now?"

"Errr, nearly, I just need to pop upstairs and change."

"Okay - ten minutes then."

Andy went upstairs hoping Jane wouldn't notice that he had taken his rucksack with him. He normally left it in the hall under the coat hooks. He quickly closed the bedroom door and took the manila envelope out of his rucksack. He carefully opened it and slid out a stack of brand new fifty-pound notes. He flicked through the crisp wad with his finger, checking that they were all genuine. He quickly counted about a quarter of them and realised that there could easily be one hundred notes inside the band, which stated five thousand pounds in large bold numerals.

He put the money back in the envelope and sat on the edge of the bed holding it to his chest. What should he do? Tell Jane how he got it? No, he decided that that wouldn't be a good idea at this stage. He got up from the bed, opened his wardrobe and pushed the envelope under his sweatshirts on the top shelf. That would have to do for now. He quickly went back downstairs and discreetly put the rucksack in its usual place under the hanging coats.

"You haven't changed," said Jane, handing Andy a chilled bottle of Budweiser.

"Decided not to in the end," Andy bluffed. "I thought I'd be comfortable enough like this. Anyway, I'm starving and the smell of that Chinese pulled me back down the stairs."

They sat at the small table in their kitchen and spent most of the time catching up with their respective news. Jane explained that she had to work late last night because a colleague was called home. His mother had had a suspected heart attack. Andy gave his opinion on architects and bricklayers. No mention of the parlous financial position they were now in. To Andy's surprise it was Jane who raised the subject first.

"Look, I'm sorry about the mess I've landed us in. You know, that credit card bill. I'll sort it, don't worry," she said.

"We'll do it together, as I said. Anyway it looks as though I could be in for a bonus soon," he said, suddenly wishing that he hadn't.

The Concrete Grave

"A bonus, what for?"

"My last project. Finished on time and made some money. Steve said he's trying to persuade Norman, our CEO, to put something through for me and Dave."

"Wow, that's good. But I don't want you to use your bonus to dig me out of a hole. There's always lots of overtime available. No one ever wants to do it, so I've already said I would."

"It'll take forever to pay that much off with just overtime. I'd like to help."

"That's really kind of you, Andy. I have been really worried about this."

"No problem," Andy replied, an uncomfortable weight settling in his stomach.

*

The alarm went off at the usual time. Andy showered and started his long trek to East London. He had slept fitfully and woke feeling more jaded than usual. He was starting to worry about Eddie and that wad of fifty-pound notes in his wardrobe. The words of his late father rang in his ears. "You never get anything for nothing in this life. There is no such thing as a free lunch." Andy shuddered as if someone had walked over his grave. He approached the site entrance; time to re-focus and concentrate on the problems of the day, and they weren't long in coming.

"We've had a call from her ladyship already," said Dave as Andy entered the office and removed his coat.

"By 'her ladyship', I presume you mean our beloved head teacher?"

"Correct," said Dave, "who else would I be referring to?"

"Oh joy. What now, she wants to invite me to coffee to commend me for the quality of our work?" retorted Andy sarcastically.

"I wish. You know that temporary waterproofing we did over the Staff Room the other day? It didn't stand up to last night's storm, the carpet and furniture are soaked and she is fuming," said Dave.

"We'd better get Tom and Jack…"

Dave held up his hand. "Already in hand. And two wet vacs have been collected and the clear up is in progress. I'd like to get that section of roof completed as soon as possible."

"Agreed. Call in Roofing Solutions, they respond quickly," said Andy who was then interrupted by the ring tone on his mobile phone. He looked at the call display screen and the word *Eddie* was flashing, Andy having added the number to his contacts. "Sorry, I'd better take this." Andy walked out of his office into the vacant room on the other side of the narrow corridor, and closed the door.

"Hello, Andy speaking."

"Andy, it's Eddie, quick question - when's that lift pit due to be concreted?"

"Lift pit? Concreted? What? Why?" Andy spluttered.

"Andy, just remember, I ask the questions, you answer them okay?" Eddie said gruffly.

"Errr, Friday morning, first thing. Two loads of ready-mixed ordered for seven thirty sharp."

"Friday. That's tomorrow."

"Correct," replied Andy somewhat cheekily.

"Well, in that case it is time you started to earn that five grand. I need you to open up tonight; or, very early tomorrow morning, to be more precise."

"Open up? Open up what?"

"The site of course, that little package I need to dispose of – it's going into your lift pit."

"Is it? I'm not sure that's possible." Andy felt his legs going weak. He pulled out a chair and sat down.

"It had better be," said Eddie, "I have invested heavily in you, Andy, and when I invest in someone I expect them to do what they're told. Get my drift? Two o'clock tomorrow morning outside the site gates it is then."

"Two o'clock - what? Why?" Andy exclaimed.

"Andy, it's much quieter at that time. You unlock the gate, let my van in and close it when we're finished. Understand?"

"Yes, okay," replied Andy as his mobile went dead. Eddie had rung off. Andy sat there, in that small office staring at his phone. It was then that he realised just how much his hand was shaking. He was jolted out of this moment of shock by shouting on the stairs; it was Dave.

"How many? Four? We need at least ten to get this job moving, you guys are having a laugh."

The Concrete Grave

Andy left the office he was in to see what the problem was. "What is it, Dave?"

"The bricklayers should be performing at The Comedy Club. Bunch of jokers. Four trowels in total with just two labourers. We need at least ten plus four or we will fall further behind programme."

"I've had enough of this. I'll call Steve. We need him to meet their Managing Director and explain a few facts of life to him, I'll do that now." Jessica, Steve's PA, explained that he was in a board meeting and Andy left a message on his mobile.

*

It was late afternoon before Steve returned Andy's call. Andy answered immediately. "Sorry, Andy, board meeting day. Started at eight this morning, still not finished. It's been painful in the extreme. I saw that I had a missed call from you, everything okay?" Steve said.

"No. It's these bricklayers, you know, the cheapest that money can buy? They're not performing and I need you to give them a good kicking," Andy said.

"Okay I'm coming up tomorrow. I'll get Tony Nugent to meet me then."

"Friday?" said Andy, "Not a good day, we've a lot happening on Friday."

"Good, I'd like to see some more happening on that site, Andy. It'll make a pleasant change." Steve was half joking in his tone, but only half.

The Concrete Grave

"But, Steve, do you really want to come here tomorrow? You know what a pain the traffic is around here on Friday afternoons," said Andy.

"Andy, what is the matter with you? I haven't been to your site for over two weeks. You've got problems and tomorrow is free. We also have a client meeting soon so I'll need to take a good look around. I'll see you first thing tomorrow." Steve was unusually short, frustration coming through in his voice.

"Okay, no worries, thanks, Steve," said Andy, worried that he'd pushed things a little too far. He was getting drawn into Eddie's plan quicker than he thought. The last thing he really wanted, with everything else going on, was his director walking onto site. He didn't want to lose his job either though, not for five thousand pounds, or was it ten? Andy had his head buried in his hands as Dave returned to the office.

"What's the matter?" he said cheerily, "It looks like you've lost a pound and found a penny."

"Steve's coming here first thing tomorrow," said Andy.

"That's good isn't it? We need him to sort out these useless bricklayers."

"Yes, of course - it's just that I've got other things on my mind."

Dave raised his eyebrows and went over to the small key cabinet on the wall and removed two bunches of keys.

"Well I'm locking up. Time to make a move," he said.

"Is it that time already?" Andy said, looking at his watch. "Six o'clock. I need a quick look round to see what we've done today." He grabbed his bright yellow safety helmet off the coat hook, put it on and quickly scampered down the stairs. His mind was filled with thoughts of that telephone conversation with Eddie. Two o'clock in the morning. How on earth was he going to explain that to Jane?

Chapter Four

Andy returned to the site office after about thirty minutes. He had his monthly progress report to prepare. These always took him an inordinate amount of time - Andy couldn't be described as academic in any way and he struggled compiling his report. He relied heavily on Jessica, Steve's PA, who knew the format of the report and could usually interpret Andy's resourceful use of the English language.

He struggled to even start the report. He couldn't concentrate. His mind was working overtime. The problems on the project seemed to pale into insignificance compared to what else was happening in his life. Also he realised he'd have to stay locally tonight. He'd almost been caught once before by train cancellations so, since then, he had kept a small overnight bag containing the essentials in the bottom drawer of the filing cabinet just in case. So far he had never used it, but tonight it would come in handy. He rang Jane and told her that he was having a curry with the team after work - team building and all that, he explained. Jane questioned the short notice and the need to stay over as Andy had never done so before. She seemed happy with his explanation that he wanted to have a few drinks with the lads tonight.

The truth was that Andy hated staying away. He never slept well in a strange bed, especially one in a Tower Hamlets bed and breakfast establishment, which by reputation were not the best in the land. He hadn't had time to book anything, but he had seen one near the site and he hoped they would have a vacant room.

It was eight thirty in the evening when Andy finally locked up and left the site, the progress report completed. After careful deliberation he had come to the conclusion that there was no easy way to tell the client that the project was now four weeks behind programme. Everything that could go wrong on a construction site had gone wrong on this one. So, he decided to be as honest and as factual as he could and would have to bear the consequences of an unhappy Local Authority who would face the prospect of having one hundred and seventy five children queued along the road with an incomplete school come the start of the new school year.

Andy headed towards Canning Town and decided to eat in the local fried chicken establishment; it didn't look great but he was hungry and it was cheap.

He sat down with his meal and paper cup containing a proprietary brand of Coke. As he munched his chips he wondered exactly what was so important about Eddie's package that he was prepared to pay an unknown person ten thousand pounds to help him dispose of it. It couldn't be too complicated though, just slip it through the reinforcing cage and tomorrow it will be underneath ten cubic metres of thirty Newton concrete.

After he'd finished eating he walked the short distance to the Bed and Breakfast that he had randomly picked. He knocked on the door and was greeted by a cheerful Bangladeshi woman in a bright yellow sari, her broad smile helped to lift the gloom that had enveloped Andy since he had left site.

"Hi," said Andy, "I was wondering whether you had a vacant room for tonight? Sorry it's such short notice, but I have had to work late."

"Of course, of course," she repeated. "We always have spare rooms. That will be forty five pounds, cash, in advance please."

Andy had no idea how much he should pay for a bed and breakfast in Tower Hamlets, or anywhere else for that matter. He took out his wallet and passed over the money.

"Thank you, sir. I'm Mrs Massoud - whatever you want, just ask," she said. She showed Andy to a room and gave him two keys on a worn piece of string. Andy explained that he would be out until quite late and Mrs Massoud explained that the second key on his key ring would unlock the front door, but added that he must make no noise at all or there would be trouble. Andy had no problem believing that in an establishment like this, that would indeed be the case.

He went into the shabby little room and closed the door. There was an overriding smell of damp and the peeling wallpaper and the torn curtains told their own story. There was a wash basin in the corner next to a rickety chest of drawers and the remainder of the room was filled by the double-bed.

Andy sat on the edge of the bed and it sank at least fifteen centimetres, the other side rising by an equal amount with the accompanying protest of old springs. He took off his boots, laid down and quickly dropped off into a dreamless sleep.

He woke with a start after hearing banging along the corridor; he quickly looked at the clock on his phone; just after midnight. Thank goodness, Andy thought. He could easily have slept past his two o'clock rendezvous; and would have done if it hadn't been for the noise created by a group of loud swearing workers stumbling along the corridor outside his room as they returned home after a night on the tiles.

Andy climbed off the bed, washed his face in cold water and waited for the allotted hour. There was no chance of any sleep from now on.

At one forty five Andy put his boots back on, gently shut his door behind him creeping downstairs as silently as possible. He was outside the site entrance within five minutes, having quickly realised that two o'clock in the morning was not the time to be hanging around on the streets in this part of East London. He had been propositioned twice, once for drugs and once for services of a sexual nature. He felt very uncomfortable waiting exposed by the site entrance.

Fortunately he did not have to wait long before a white transit van pulled up. Eddie climbed out of the passenger side and greeted Andy like a long lost friend; Andy struggled to return the compliment.

"Andy, great to see you, how's it going?" he said, as if he was walking into the wedding reception of his best friend.

"Fine, thanks, considering it's two in the morning, I'm freezing, and wishing I was tucked up in bed. What do you want me to do?"

The Concrete Grave

"Unlock the gates, open them, and when the van has driven in, close them and show us where to go."

Two other men climbed out and Andy suddenly got even more nervous than he had been five minutes earlier. The team was certainly slick and before he knew it, the white van was reversing onto the site and he was pulling the gates shut behind them. He hoped that no one would notice the fact that the padlock was not in position, at that moment it was in his jacket pocket.

"Woa!" Eddie said in a strangely moderate voice, the van was within three metres of the lift pit and as close as it could get.

"Right, Tone, open the doors and let's get this done pronto," Eddie said.

By now Andy was level with the back of the van just as the three men were struggling with what looked like a huge tree trunk in the dark.

"What the ……," spluttered Andy in complete shock. Upon closer inspection he could see that Eddie's 'package' was six foot long and wrapped in a black tarpaulin sheet held together with black duct tape.

"You said a small package," said Andy, "how the hell do you think you are going to get that in there?" Andy pointed at the steel reinforcement cage sitting in the bottom of the hole.

"Be prepared, is what I learnt in the Boy Scouts," said the man Andy now knew to be Tone, he was brandishing a pair of steel fixers nips in one hand and a roll of tying wire in the other.

"You are not touching that," said Andy, referring to the reinforcement cage, and surprising himself with the ferocity of his comment, "that's all been signed off by the Clerk of Works."

"We are," replied Eddie, "and you've no need to worry. Tone used to be a steel fixer until he saw the light and joined my company."

By this time Tone had clambered on to the top of the cage and was expertly cutting through the tying wire holding the top layer of reinforcement bars in position. Within two minutes the top layer was removed and carefully stacked at the edge of the excavation. Tone returned to join Eddie and the other man, who was still nameless as far as Andy was concerned, to help them with the bundle, as 'package' had clearly been an inappropriate term.

"This is not a *small package*," said Andy, stating the blindingly obvious in a final and pointless show of resistance.

"Small, large - what's the difference? We're here, and you're here with us; how you gonna explain that one then?" Eddie said.

Andy knew that Eddie had a point; he put his hand to his forehead and groaned. He then turned his attention to the bundle which was being expertly manoeuvred towards the hole. Eddie had taken a large torch out of the van and was pointing it carefully in the general direction of the lift pit. Andy wasn't normally slow on the uptake, but then again he wasn't usually standing on his construction site in the early hours of the morning with three men who would sell their own grandmother for a fiver.

The Concrete Grave

The dawning of realisation was confirmed at almost the same time as the man with no name slipped and dropped the side of the bundle he was holding.

"Taff, you plonker," exclaimed Eddie, so at least Andy knew the missing name now. That was nothing to match the shock that surged through Andy's frame as he saw a human arm fall out between the layers of tarpaulin. The hand attached to the arm was unusual too as the four fingers could be clearly seen in the torchlight but the thumb of the right hand was very definitely missing.

"Tie that back and get this lump into that hole," said Eddie.

Andy stood motionless; he couldn't have moved even if he had wanted to. The penny had completely dropped now. He was just beginning to realise what he was getting himself mixed up in, and began to understand why he would be ten thousand pounds richer by the end of the evening; a realisation that made him feel extremely uncomfortable.

The wrapped body was by now being carefully positioned on to the bottom layer of reinforcement, against the side of the excavation. In this light Andy was impressed, as it was barely visible from the top of the pit. Whether it would be visible tomorrow morning would be another matter. By that time Eddie, Tone and Taff would be long gone and he would be overseeing the concrete pour.

Tone quickly replaced the top layer of reinforcement bars and Andy had to acknowledge that he had done a good job, probably better than the original.

The Concrete Grave

"If you want a job tomorrow, Tone, pop in and we'll sort you out," Andy joked - no one laughed and he regretted the comment as soon as it had left his lips.

As the three men returned to the van Andy turned to Eddie, "What if it's seen tomorrow?"

"That, my man, is your problem - but hopefully with the concrete arriving first thing he'll be gone by lunchtime. Now open the gate for us there's a good chap," replied Eddie slapping a package into Andy's chest; Andy's hand automatically went to hold the envelope as Eddie jumped into the van which was already making its way towards the gate.

Andy ran beside the van and quickly swung open the gates; the van drove out, Andy closed the gates and snapped the padlock into the staple. He looked up as the van drove down the road, and he couldn't help noticing the last three letters on the number plate: GON. Gone by lunchtime. How appropriate, thought Andy.

As he made his way back to Mrs Massoud's B & B he looked at his watch, twelve minutes past two, just over ten minutes and the job was done, slick work – they have probably done it before, Andy thought. One grand per minute - the best rate he'd ever been paid. But, as he walked up the cold misty street he had a horrible hollow feeling in the pit of his stomach. He had to be back there on site in less than five hours, he knew what the others didn't know and he was starting to feel distinctly nervous.

Andy barely slept, the bed was uncomfortable, there was continuous noise from outside his window as well as from inside the house; but it wasn't that that kept him awake, it was the gradual realisation of the enormity of what he had done. As he lay there various thoughts came rushing into his head. He was complicit now; he had been paid for concealing a body. He was, what do they call it? An accessory, that's it, an accessory; he had no idea how he had so rapidly become part of this. He felt physically sick and he knew deep down that this was unlikely to be the end of the episode.

*

Andy woke just before six o'clock; he was surprised by his surroundings and it took him several seconds to work out where he was. His alarm had been set for six thirty but he knew he wouldn't get back to sleep now. He washed and shaved and decided to skip Mrs Massoud's breakfast; for some reason he didn't feel very hungry. As he had paid the night before he had no reason to see anyone and, in view of his nocturnal activities, he decided it was best to be seen by as few people as possible.

He reached the site entrance just before seven o'clock and was unlocking the padlock for the second time that day just as Dave was turning the corner.

"Blimey, Andy, you wet the bed or something?" Dave said, "We don't see you around at this time normally."

"Very funny. No, I stayed over - by the time I finished that progress report I couldn't face the long journey home so I stayed at a local B & B."

"Not Mrs Massoud's I hope," said Dave.

"Yes, as a matter of fact it was, why?"

"You didn't have the breakfast did you?" smiled Dave.

"No, I didn't," said Andy as Dave marched towards the office.

"Then you've only the bedbugs to worry about." Dave said as he made his way up the stairs.

"Since when did you become an expert on B & B's in Tower Hamlets?" said Andy a few minutes later, as he took a sip from the mug of coffee the Dave had made for him.

"I'm not, but everyone knows not to stay at Mrs Massoud's, the lads steer well clear."

"Thanks for nothing," said Andy, as he heard a large loud engine noise from outside the site office window.

"Concrete's here early," said Dave, "That's good, we can get cracking."

Andy was pleased, it was not yet dawn and the darker it stayed for the first part of the pour the better. He grabbed his fluorescent jacket and helmet. "I'll come and check all is okay," he said.

"No need," said Dave "You stay here and drink your coffee, I've got everything under control."

Andy knew that he would have, but there was no way he was going to miss the first load of concrete going into that hole. By the time he reached the excavated lift pit, the ready mixed concrete lorry had reversed close to the edge of the excavated hole and the vehicle was stationary with the engine running. The driver was positioning his chute, he pulled a small lever on the side of the vehicle and, as the drum started turning, concrete flowed down the chute and through the top level of reinforcement and quickly started filling up the hole. Andy was terrified; he wondered whether bodies floated in concrete? He'd already worked out that he'd have to plead ignorance if anything untoward was spotted. Within ten minutes the load was fully discharged, the hole was half full and any possible chance of the buried body being found had gone for ever. Andy breathed a sigh of relief, too loudly as it happened.

"What's up?" Dave said.

"Nothing, nothing. It's just good to get this pour out of the way so we can start erecting those wall shutters on Monday," he replied.

"Yeh, need to get this end of the job moving. Be all finished by lunchtime at this rate," said Dave.

Andy almost ran back to the office, he was so relieved at the way things had turned out. His relative levity was brought to a sudden halt when he saw Steve, his contracts director, just walking into the office and taking his off coat. Andy had completely forgotten that Steve was visiting today and he felt the blood drain from his face. Steve was always smartly dressed, wearing a suit and a tie even though it was Friday. His fashionable glasses made his look studious, although he was the most experienced construction employee in the company. He was a man of integrity, a 'people person' and very popular with all of his team who would always go that extra mile for him.

"Hello, Andy, what's up?" Steve said.

"Hi, Steve, nothing really, I stayed over that's all. I had to work late to finish the Progress Report. Spent the night

The Concrete Grave

at Mrs Massoud's B & B, which according to Dave is inhabited by several species of bedbugs. I didn't sleep very well."

"Sounds charming," said Steve, "Remind me not to stay there if ever I have to stay up this way. I'm impressed though, I thought you didn't like sleeping in strange beds." After working with Andy for over twenty years Steve knew him very well.

"I don't," Andy replied, "But needs must. Coffee, Steve?"

"Yes please, and then we'll have a look around outside. Good to see that lift pit being concreted."

"Yes, certainly is," replied Andy, hoping that he didn't sound too relieved.

After they finished their coffee Andy showed Steve around site. When he reached the far corner Steve turned towards Andy and said; "Is everything all right, Andy? You haven't seemed your old self these past few days and you were very strange on the phone yesterday; it was as if you were trying to hide something. That's unlike you."

Just then Andy's phone echoed to the text received alert, he quickly glanced at the sender and he saw that it was Eddie. He opened the text; it simply read:

All okay?

Andy quickly put the phone back in his pocket.

"No, no," Andy stammered, "Everything's fine. Well, apart from trying to keep this job on programme. We've got an architect who couldn't design a toilet block for a scout camp and a bricklayer who can't lay bricks. Apart from that, all's well."

"Okay, well I'm meeting Tony Nugent at nine; we'll see what he's got to say for himself. So long as you're okay. Everything all right at home?" Steve said.

"Yes, fine thanks, couldn't be better," Andy said, hating himself for lying to the person who had helped him so much during his career.

Steve left site just after lunch. The meeting with the Managing Director of the bricklaying sub-contractor appeared to have gone well, lots of promises for extra bricklayers for next week, although Andy doubted whether there would be much change. He donned his site helmet and left the office to check on progress of the concreting of the lift pit. As he arrived the ground workers were tamping the surface with a long length of timber, job just about finished. Andy stood staring at the operation, unable to stop thinking about the body of the man at the bottom of all that concrete.

"You all right, Andy?" he hadn't seen Dave creep up on him.

"Yes, why shouldn't I be?" Andy said.

"It's just that you seem to be taking an unnatural interest in the concreting of that lift pit."

"Just keeping an eye on progress. Okay?" Suddenly the pressures of the last few days finally got to Andy and he turned to Dave, put his nose with a few inches of Dave's face and bellowed, "I am the bloody project manager. Have you got a problem?"

"Okay, okay, calm down, I was only making an observation." Dave said as he moved away rapidly to check up on the bricklayers.

Andy quickly realised that he shouldn't have been so short with Dave and he had already decided to apologise to him when he came back to the office.

"I'm sorry, Dave; I didn't mean to snap at you earlier," Andy said when he returned.

"That's okay; you're tired after a busy week, especially with that lack of sleep from your night spent at Mrs Massoud's. Hey, why don't you leave early? It's Friday after all, give Jane a surprise." Dave said.

"Hmmm, not a bad idea, I might just do that; I'm totally knackered and not much is happening this afternoon."

Andy left the site just after three o'clock, only too pleased to be putting a dreadful week behind him. He thought of Eddie and his text, and realised he hadn't yet replied; this gave him a surprising feeling of power, although with Steve on site he'd completely forgotten. He put his hands in his pockets as he walked towards Canning Town tube station, he felt the bulk of the second envelope Eddie had given him, and surprisingly he felt slightly better.

The Concrete Grave

Chapter Five

Andy had what could best be described as a quiet weekend. Jane was working away again and he decided that he didn't want to do much. He didn't want to see anybody. He was tired, very tired. The stress of the past few days had brought a heavy toll on his body and he felt it. He had a few beers, drank most of a bottle of white wine on Friday night and slept in on Saturday morning. When he awoke he still didn't feel much better.

He did do a few odd jobs around the house on Saturday. He fitted a shelf in the bathroom and a picture that needed hanging in the hall. The afternoon was spent in front of the television watching Sky Sports as the goals were reported from the Saturday afternoon football matches. His mood was not helped by his beloved Liverpool losing once again.

Andy was aware that his mind was otherwise occupied. The main problem he had now was what to do with his cash. Suddenly he had ten thousand pounds in fifty-pound notes and what was he going to do with it? He'd heard from friends that he couldn't just pay the money into his bank; there were regulations to prevent money laundering apparently. He spent some time researching on the Internet what he could do, and quickly learned that large cash sums paid into a bank without a receipt or an audit trail were often reported or even rejected. It seemed that the only solution was a safety deposit box at Waterloo station or a trip to Switzerland with a briefcase full of money, neither of which appealed much to Andy.

Sunday was even quieter than Saturday, another long lie in followed by a fried breakfast. He walked to the local newsagent to buy the Sunday papers and spent the afternoon on the settee reading them from cover to cover.

*

Andy hated Mondays, probably more than most people did. It meant another early alarm call and the trains always seemed to fill up on Mondays more than on any other day of the week. He grabbed his copy of *The Metro* and fell asleep in his usual window seat.

He arrived on site with no enthusiasm at all and made himself a large cup of coffee to help ease his way into what was inevitably going to be another hectic week on site. He casually flicked through the pages of his unread copy of *The Metro* and as he turned to page four his heart almost stopped; the headline shouting at him read:

East End gangster missing: Presumed dead

Andy quickly read the article:

It has been reported that the renowned East End Godfather, Tommy Sutcliffe has not been seen for several days. He was reported missing on Tuesday last week and close contacts of Tommy have expressed their concern as to his exact whereabouts.

Tommy Sutcliffe has built up an empire of illegal dealings over the past twenty five years. Sutcliffe was known as 'One Thumb Tommy' due to the fact that the thumb on his right hand was removed, apparently chopped off whilst being tortured by a member of an opposition gang.

Andy could not believe what he had read. One thumb could only mean one thing, the person at the bottom of his lift shaft was not just anybody; it was Tommy Sutcliffe.

"Good morning, Andy. How are you feeling now after the weekend?" Dave said. "I said, how are you feeling, Andy?" Dave repeated after a thirty second silence. Andy slowly looked up from the paper and stared blankly at Dave.

"Oh, sorry, Dave, I was thinking about something else," Andy said.

"I should think you were, I take it that the answer to my original question is 'no better' then. It looks as though you've just seen a ghost, not much change from when you left on Friday afternoon. A heavy weekend I assume?" Dave continued.

"No, not really," said Andy, "it's just that I'm worried about this job; I'm just thinking about the programme and how we can recover the time we've lost so far."

"It looks more like you're reading the paper to me," said Dave, "unless you use *The Metro* for inspiration on how to recover a four week delay in the next six weeks."

"Yes, well, anyway how was your weekend?" Andy said trying quickly to change the subject.

"Not too bad, my daughter came round with that useless boyfriend of hers. We didn't do much else."

Andy quickly finished his cup of coffee, put on his site helmet and coat and started to leave the office, "I'm just going to take a quick look round and check that everything's alright for the start of the new week." The truth was that Andy couldn't wait to get out of the office and conclude the conversation he was having. He needed time to think further on the ramifications of what he had just read in the paper. Could it really be the body of one of the foremost gangsters from the East End of London in the bottom of his lift pit? What should he do now? Who should he approach? He really had no idea, and decided that the only option was to concentrate on solving the problems that his job presented him with.

*

Less than five miles away as the crow flies, in a very small and dark office sat Detective Chief Inspector Jeremy Lloyd-Brown. Detective Chief Inspector Lloyd-Brown wasn't your typical DCI; he didn't look like one, and he'd had a very different upbringing from most other serving police officers of high rank. His father and his grandfather had both made personal fortunes from the world of merchant banking. Jeremy was educated at Eton and followed his grandfather and father by going to Downing College, Cambridge, where he studied philosophy. In theory, his career path was set out before him. He would join his father's merchant bank and would reach the position of Chief Executive by the age of forty. But Jeremy had different ideas; he was strong willed and had always had a desire to serve in the police force, so as soon as he left Cambridge he enrolled into Hendon Police College, much to the dismay of his parents. His obvious talents soon set him apart and he was fast tracked through officer training becoming the youngest Detective Chief Inspector in Britain by the age of thirty-six.

Another thing that set Lloyd-Brown apart from his peers was that he was very popular with the men he commanded; affable and fair but firm was the best way to describe his approach to man management. He'd often join his men in the local pub for a drink at the end of the day; he knew the first names of all the wives, partners and children of his men and that went a long way. Most of his team would run through walls for DCI Jeremy Lloyd-Brown.

The office was small and had clearly once been part of a much bigger room; the plasterboard partition cut through the ornate fibrous plaster cornice at the ceiling which gave it an awkward feel of being just a slice of a room, taller than it was long. It had a disproportionately sized window covered by a plain beige blind that was half way up the window and looked as though it hadn't been moved for years. The office was just big enough for a chair and desk with another small chair in front of that, which just fitted into the cluttered floor space.

Jeremy Lloyd-Brown cut a dashing figure; he always dressed very smartly in a dark pinstripe suit that was tailor-made not off the peg, with a silk handkerchief poking out of the top pocket, a dazzling white shirt and a flamboyant tie. He looked strangely at odds with his surroundings, an impression that was made a good deal stronger by the fluorescent pink tie he had chosen to wear that morning. He was head of the OCU, the Organised Crime Unit. This small group of just six people was little known in the Metropolitan Police Force, and that was the way the Commissioner wanted things to stay. Their job was to monitor gangland activity in London; which usually meant that most of their time was spent in the East End of London. Most people thought that organised crime had died with the Crays. It hadn't; it was still alive and kicking, and Jeremy Lloyd-Brown's sole personal mission was to ensure that any gangland activity was kept to a bare minimum.

There was a loud bang at the door and, without waiting for any response, a large curly haired man burst his way into the office.

"Jez, have you heard?" Jeremy Lloyd-brown insisted that everybody from the tea lady to the Chief Superintendent called him Jez; he was different and wanted people to know that.

"Yes I've heard; Tommy Sutcliffe is missing presumed dead, I was tipped off last Wednesday that this could be the case. Apparently he left to go for dinner with friends and never arrived; where he is now is anyone's guess. Probably done a runner, Tommy's too smart to get himself topped." Jez replied in a deep voice that could only have been cultivated in the hallowed classrooms of Eton College.

"Do you think that he knew we were onto him?" Detective Constable Toby West asked.

"I don't see how; but he has informers everywhere so that may be the case. Probably sunning himself on some Brazilian beach by now," Jez said.

"That makes three gangland leaders that have gone missing in eighteen months, doesn't it?" Toby said.

"Four in two years if you count Brendan Codner," Jez replied.

"Oh, yes, I forgot about him, never found the perpetrator there either did we?" Toby said.

"No, and I doubt if we ever will."

"What do we do now, sit and wait?"

"No, we need to take a proactive approach. Keep a close watch on that pile of his in Essex. See who comes in and goes out. Let me know immediately if he is spotted. If he is, then the whole thing's a false alarm. If he's not; who knows?"

Jez got up from his seat and almost pushed past West; he grabbed his coat from a hook on the wall and went out of the office. "I've got a meeting with the Chief Super, you and Roger stake out his house, okay?"

With that Lloyd-Brown was gone and West turned and went back to his desk and rang Roger Steele to give him the news.

*

"An integrity test. What the hell is an integrity test and why does that gormless Engineer want to do one on my site?" screamed Andy.

"Well according to Rudolph – at least his parents had a sense of humour - it is a sonic test to show whether there are any cracks or voids in any of the foundations," Dave replied calmly.

The Concrete Grave

"How does it work? I've not had to do one before."

"Well, basically someone whacks the top of the concrete and this clever bit of kit records the sound waves going down and coming back up. If there isn't a regular flow it means there's a crack or void in the concrete. We get a pretty little graph to show for our six hundred and fifty quid," said Dave as he backed quickly out of the site office as he knew what Andy would do next.

"How much? Are you mad, we don't have six hundred and fifty quid to pay someone to hit our concrete foundations with a bloody hammer. And where pray tell, are they expecting to do this; all our foundations have brickwork built on them or are backfilled," said Andy.

"Oh, no worries there, I said we could do it on the lift shaft base; we can still easily get to that. Anyway, it's all arranged, I set it up on Friday evening, after you'd gone home; the men will be here any minute."

At that precise moment Andy had chosen to take a mouthful of coffee, his mug was still close to his mouth when Dave uttered that last sentence and over half of the contents were effectively jettisoned across the office in the direction of Dave, who moved to his left swiftly as the spray sailed past him and towards the open door.

"You told him what? No, no, no. We are not doing it. Can't afford it, it will delay the job and it seems a pointless waste of time to me," Andy said once he had recovered from his choking fit.

"Apparently it is in the specification that we must do at least one integrity test. I've done it on piles before but not a solid base. But our friend Rudolph says do it, or break up the lift pit."

"He can't say that. Can he?" Andy said.

"He's the Engineer; he can say anything he likes really. The fact that we haven't priced it is not his fault and is not his problem. He can make life very difficult for us if we don't do what he says."

Andy could only drop his head into his hands and let out a loud groan; surely his situation couldn't get much worse. But he was wrong, things could get much worse he realised as his mobile phone rang and it was Eddie. Andy looked at his illuminated screen as if it were the world's largest poisonous spider; he instinctively answered it and Dave used it as his excuse to make a rapid exit.

"Eddie, long time, no speak. What can I do for you?" Andy said in a far cheerier manner than he felt.

"Andy, my boy. I just wanted to see how you were," Eddie said in a matter of fact voice.

"That's very nice of you, Eddie," Andy said sarcastically. "Very caring, nice to see there are some responsible employers still around. I have just discovered that your 'package' was the body of one of the biggest names in the East End underworld, how the hell do you think I am?"

"Ahh, so you know," Eddie said in a somewhat disappointed tone.

"Yes, I do know, couldn't really have missed it could I? It's plastered all over the pages of every national newspaper in the country."

"Calm down, Andy, there's no need to get excited now."

"No need to get excited, are you kidding? I've half a mind to go straight to Scotland Yard and tell them what you've done," Andy said, immediately regretting it as soon as he said it.

"Tell them what *I've* done?" Eddie said, with the emphasis on the 'I've'. "What *you've* done more like, how do you think you'll get out of this if you come clean? It won't be simple as that, it'll be ten years for you, and believe me you won't like life in Wormwood Scrubs, that's for certain." Andy was silent for a few moments while he let Eddie's comments sink in. He realised that he needed to placate him, however strongly he felt. He was terrified and angering Eddie at this juncture was not the way to go.

"Okay, okay, I'm not going anywhere and I've got a job to do. So if you don't mind I'll say goodbye." At that Andy disconnected the call. He looked at his hand, it was shaking violently; he wasn't sure what he was going to do.

"The guys are here to do the integrity test, Andy." Andy hadn't noticed Dave coming up behind him and had forgotten about the earlier shock, which was superseded by another when Eddie had rung.

"I told you, we're not doing it," Andy said, fearful of what the results may show. The game would then be well and truly up.

"Well, you'd better explain that to Rudolph," said Dave, "I can't see for the life of me what your problem is. They have already started and they have said it'll take less

The Concrete Grave

than an hour. I say get it done and we can move on." Dave said feeling more and more frustrated.

"All done, Dave," said a voice that Andy did not recognise.

"What's 'all done?'" questioned Andy.

"The integrity test, guv, all finished. I told Dave that it wouldn't take long. No problems, it's all fine." The man was from Sonic Images, the company that conducted the test.

"All fine did you say?" Andy said, open mouthed.

"Yes, clean as a whistle," said the man.

"Oh, great, well so it should be," Andy said, not believing his luck.

As the test team left site Dave went up to Andy and said, "What was your problem with that test? I told you it would be a formality."

"Don't like being ripped off that's all. Six hundred and fifty quid for fifteen minutes work? It's a con, plain and simple. I'll tell Accounts not to pay them." Andy said.

The remainder of the day flew by; Mondays were always busy, with time sheets to do, finishing last week's progress diary for the office, as well as updating the programme. Andy also had a meeting with the window supplier This turned out to be more bad news as he was advised that, due to a global shortage of aluminium, the delivery for his windows would now be twelve weeks and not the previously promised eight, as stated in the original quotation. Just what he didn't need as getting the building watertight was critical to commencing the internal finishes and achieving completion.

It was almost six o'clock and as Dave was putting his coat on he said, "By the way Brian Hay rang earlier, he wants to do a QA audit on Friday."

"That's all we need," said Andy. "You know how much work we have to do to prepare for one of those? Can you start checking things over tomorrow, Dave? We don't need a failed QA audit; the ramifications can be extremely painful, as you well know."

Quality assurance audits were the bane of every project manager's life. An independent department was charged with the responsibility for ensuring that the managers working on site followed the prescribed procedures. They made it their personal mission to find fault with what the site team were doing. If the audit failed to achieve at least seventy five per cent it led to a visit from the Managing Director who was then responsible for ensuring that the site team closed out all the non-conformances within seven days.

"Will do, I'll speak to Sue tomorrow. When I turn on the charm she'll become putty in my hand. I'm off, see you tomorrow."

Sue Patmore was the Assistant Auditor and both Andy and Dave knew the value of keeping on the right side of her. Giving her a box of chocolates every Christmas was a small price to pay for a score of seventy six per cent on their projects.

"Yes, thanks, Dave, have a good evening," replied Andy.

Andy locked up the site gates just as it started to rain on what was already a cold, dark November evening. He

The Concrete Grave

trudged towards Canning Town tube station, his mind in a whirl following today's revelations. He was so engrossed in his own thoughts that he did not hear the two large men approach from behind. The first thing that Andy knew of their intentions was when a heavy blow struck the back of his head. The explosion of light that burst across his eyes was accompanied by a tidal wave of pain, and he fell to the pavement like a sack of potatoes. Landing face down on the wet tarmac Andy was vaguely aware of the fingers rifling through the inside of his coat, but he was too weak to do anything about it. It was a matter of seconds before he was overcome by a shroud of blackness.

"You alright mate? Looks like you've taken a tumble."

Andy couldn't make out the blurred face above him and as he tried to lift his head from the damp pavement, he stopped immediately, overcome by intense pain and nausea.

"Don't move, we've called an ambulance, they'll be here in a minute," said the friendly, but concerned voice.

As Andy put his head down he was aware that some kind soul had put something soft under his head as he slipped back into unconsciousness.

"Can you tell me your name?" an authoritative voice said. Andy opened his eyes to see a uniformed paramedic in front of him with a latex gloved hand either side of his head, clearly trying to prevent him from moving.

"We're just checking you over and we'll get you into the ambulance pronto. Do you remember where you are?" The voice asked.

Andy tried to recall where he was and how he got there.

"No, I was walking along, now I'm here and my head feels like it has split in two," he groaned. "My name's Andy, if that helps."

"Well, Andy, it looks like you've been mugged, anything missing?"

Andy felt the weight of his backpack still on his back, and slowly felt his inside pocket.

"My phone, it's gone."

"Yeh, that's usual. An iPhone was it? Very popular with the muggers round here, they are. Stay still while we lift you on the stretcher; we'll get you to A & E as soon as we can."

"Where are you taking me? I need to get home," Andy slurred.

"You are having a little trip with us to Bart's Hospital first. They'll check you over, then you'll be on your way," said the reassuring voice. As Andy felt the vehicle move off he heard the wail of a siren, saw the reflection of the flashing blue light and decided to lay back and close his eyes.

He was aroused from his semi-conscious state by the vibrations as he was loaded on to a trolley and whisked through the waiting crowds in the Accident and Emergency Department at St. Bartholomew's Hospital. Andy had no idea what time it was but he was surprised by the number of people waiting to be seen. He had little time to think about it as he was whisked into a curtained cubicle to be seen by a large smiling West Indian nurse. The first words that the nurse said filled Andy with dread.

"There are two police officers waiting to see you; do you feel well enough to speak to them?"

"Err, no, why?" said Andy filled with panic. They must have found the body was his initial thought.

"They want to ask you a few questions about the mugging," she replied.

Of course, Andy realised, his guilty conscience getting the better of him once again.

"Yes, why not?" he said drearily.

Andy found the ordeal of answering the questions from the police officers harder than he thought, as he struggled to keep his brain working properly. They took his personal details and the details of his stolen mobile phone, but he was not much help other than that. He had seen nothing and, as he understood it, there were no witnesses either. It was therefore highly unlikely that the police would catch the culprits.

"That's enough now," said the cheerful nurse, "I need to check him over."

Andy was relieved to see the two police officers leave the hospital, clearly realising that they were unlikely to find anything more that would be much use to them. But just as they were leaving he heard one of them say, "Strange, muggers wouldn't normally target someone as big and fit as him - they must have been desperate."

Andy lay on the uncomfortable trolley for what seemed like hours to eventually be seen by a young female doctor who didn't look old enough to have left school, let alone university. She introduced herself as Emma. She was very polite and remarkably efficient, but insisted that he had to have a scan of his head. This was done surprisingly quickly and twenty minutes after the results came through he was told that there was no obvious damage. He was told that he would be given a prescription for painkillers and he would then be free to go home.

The nurse he saw when he arrived came up to him smiling, "You'll live," she said handing him the prescription for strong painkillers. "You have already had two of these; they should last until you get home, then take two more every four hours. You've had a nasty bump on the head, so take care."

"Thanks," said Andy, as he gingerly got up from the bed. As he stood he felt decidedly wobbly, but managed to start walking towards the exit.

"And take tomorrow off work; that knock on the head will take some time to settle down."

Some hope of that thought Andy. He couldn't leave Dave on his own, not with the project as it is.

Andy asked for directions to the nearest tube station and made his way towards the Barbican, 'five minutes' walk' the eastern European man on reception had told him. But it took Andy almost fifteen minutes; and he was relieved to make it.

Andy suddenly realised that he hadn't told Jane what had happened and went to take his phone out of his pocket before remembering that he no longer had his mobile phone.

The Concrete Grave

He'd have to call her from Waterloo. Do they even have public phone boxes these days? Andy wondered. Surely everyone has a mobile phone now; everyone except him that is.

Andy got on the nine fifteen train, almost three hours later than usual. As the train pulled out of the station he remembered that he had not looked for a phone box and hadn't called Jane. Never mind he thought, she expects me to be late most nights and hopefully I have a good enough excuse this time.

As the grubby London suburbs flashed past the window Andy thought about the incident and the comment made by the police officer as he was leaving the hospital. "*Muggers wouldn't normally target someone as big and young as him,*" he'd said. Was this a random mugging? Or was it related to the events of the last week? It was only this morning that he had made the ill-advised comment to Eddie that he would go to Scotland Yard. No, surely he was being paranoid, but he had a growing knot of worry in his stomach that he was involved in something far bigger than he was able to cope with. He closed his eyes and dropped into a groggy semi-sleep.

It was almost eleven o'clock when Andy got home; the house was in darkness. As he unlocked the front door, he did so quietly, assuming that Jane had taken an early night and was in bed. His head was agony now and all he had in his pocket was the prescription that the nurse had given to him. He hadn't even thought of finding a chemist. He'd have to make do with paracetamol from the bathroom cabinet for now.

He crept upstairs, but Jane was not there and the house was empty. That's strange, thought Andy; Jane always lets me know if she's working late, she'd always send me a text. Again, he realised how reliant he was on his mobile phone. How do people manage without them?

Andy was drained and exhausted so he decided to undress and take a quick shower; he was filthy from lying on that East London pavement. After taking two painkillers he climbed into bed and within seconds he had drifted into a deep and dreamless sleep.

Chapter Six

Andy awoke with the early morning sunlight shining through the gap in the curtains. He looked at the alarm clock. It was eight thirty-five in the morning. He hadn't set the alarm before he went to sleep and he had overslept by over three hours.

Andy quickly got out of bed and stopped as if he'd been hit on the head by a cricket bat. His head was splitting and he quickly recalled the events of the previous evening. He felt dizzy and sick and the depression that he had felt over the past few days came swiftly back to him. He surprised himself by the suddenness of his decision that he would not be going to work immediately, not until the afternoon at the earliest.

He had to ring Steve and let him know. Then, not for the first time, he remembered that he did not have his mobile phone and because he and Jane both owned mobile phones they did not have a landline in the house either. He'd have to find a phone box in the village. He was sure he'd seen one somewhere.

He dressed, took two more painkillers and drove about one mile before he found a phone box. He put in a one pound coin and called the office, one of the few telephone numbers he knew off by heart. He explained to Steve what had happened the previous evening in some detail, embellishing in places for dramatic effect.

"That's terrible," said Steve sympathetically. "What a dump that part of London is, scumbags everywhere. What can I do to help?"

"Well, I'll need a replacement phone I'm afraid, as soon as possible as I'm lost without it. I'll try to get to site by early afternoon." Andy said.

"No you won't. You'll spend today at home at least. It sounds as though you've got concussion. What did the hospital say?"

"Not much, they gave me a prescription and told me to rest, not sure for how long. Okay, I'll be back tomorrow all being well," Andy said.

Once Steve had hung up, he rang Jane's mobile, it went straight to voicemail so he left a brief message explaining what had happened and that he hoped to see her tonight.

Andy called into the chemist on the way home to get the prescription painkillers, he bought a paper and went back home. He was exhausted and scared; the unexpected free day would at least give him some time to think things through and attempt to come up with a plan.

Andy tried to read the paper and watch some day time television but his mind kept taking him back to the situation he was in. He just didn't know what to do. He knew that he had done wrong and essentially he was a moral person. Confronting Eddie wouldn't help, nor could he go to the police as he supposed that he would be the only one in the dock. By the end of the day he was still no nearer a plan than he was when he awoke.

*

The Concrete Grave

At that moment in time, outside a large house on the outskirts of Buckhurst Hill in Essex, DC's West and Steele were sitting in a nondescript Ford Focus parked just off the road within sight of a pair of huge iron gates which were fixed on to two very grand brick pillars. The mansion they were watching belonged to Tommy Sutcliffe.

"This is a total waste of time," said Roger Steele. "It is surely obvious he's either gone or a gonna. Either way he is not likely to be driving in or out of these gates. We've been sat here for almost twelve hours."

"You know what the essence of surveillance is, don't you?" Toby said.

"Yeh, patience," said Roger, somewhat aggressively.

"Correct, patience."

"Well mine's now gone. I suggest we call Jez and either get a relief team, or we go home and get some sleep." Roger said.

"A relief team? What planet are you on? You know there are only six of us altogether. Everyone is flat out; where do you think a relief team will come from?" Toby said with an incredulous tone.

"So, home for some kip then? Twelve hour shifts can damage your health. They may be alright for Jack Bauer, but not for me," Roger joked.

"Well, as you've been snoring away for the best part of three hours I doubt if you will pass the audition for the part of Jack Bauer," Toby countered.

"Well, errr, I'm worried about your health, Toby," Roger said, reverting to a more apologetic tone now.

"Very kind, but I do agree, time to call Jez and see what he wants us to do."

The call to Jez took less than two minutes.

"Good news," reported Toby as he put his mobile phone back into the top pocket of his jacket. "Kip time it is. Jez agrees that we've done enough."

"That's good, let's get out of here."

Just as West was about to turn the ignition key, the huge electronic gates started to open slowly and a red van passed them and turned into the long drive. Debut Domestic Cleaning Services was sign written in white on the side of the van.

"Interesting, looks like Mrs Mopp has arrived," said Roger.

"Make a note of the name; we'll pay them a visit later, they may be able to help us."

West started the engine of the Ford Focus and the two detectives drove back to London for some well-earned rest.

*

Andy's headache lasted throughout Tuesday. The pain slightly eased for a couple of hours after he had taken the painkillers, but not by much.

By ten o'clock in the evening there was still no sign of Jane. This wasn't unusual with the job she had, but given the circumstances over the past twenty four hours, Andy was getting extremely concerned. Andy checked his personal email address, but nothing. He decided he'd make every effort to get to work the next day so he set the alarm for five am and had an early night.

When the alarm went off the next morning Andy felt slightly better; he still had a slight headache and that gnawing feeling in the pit of his stomach was still there but there was no reason not to return to work. He took two painkillers just in case and headed for East London feeling ready for action.

As usual he was greeted by Dave as he walked into the site office, which was strewn with drawings over every worktop and a good number on the floor too. The place was a complete mess.

"Blimey, Dave, I'm gone for one day and you turn the office into a scene from *Apocalypse Now*."

"Yeh, sorry, Andy, I was looking for the first floor window details. The bricklayers wanted the opening sizes," Dave said defensively.

Andy walked smartly over to the drawing rack at the far side of the office, stepping over and around the drawings strewn across the floor. He counted three clips back, pulled out a set of twenty drawings and laid them across his desk. He flicked through half a dozen drawings.

"This one?" he said revealing a drawing showing the elevations.

"Yup, that's it, thanks," Dave said.

"Dave, you need to learn where the drawings are, and you'd better tidy up this office smartish." Andy said.

"I was just about to do it when you walked in. I wasn't really expecting you today. Steve told me what happened, are you okay now?" Dave said sympathetically.

"Well, okay might be going a bit far, but I'm better than I was yesterday that's for sure."

"What happened exactly, Steve was a bit vague on the phone."

"Well, to be honest I'm not sure; I was walking along Lavender Avenue…"

"The dark one?" Dave interrupted.

"Yes, the dark one, and the next thing I knew I was on the deck with the mother and father of all headaches."

"There have been a lot of muggings around here, *Muggers Paradise* they call it," Dave said.

"Who calls it *Muggers Paradise?*"

"Well, I do for one."

"I suppose I have no reason to argue with that, have I?" said Andy.

"What did they take?"

"Well, that's the strange thing, I had my laptop in my backpack and my wallet in my back pocket but they only took my phone."

"I've heard that you can get a hundred quid for a decent iPhone in the pub."

"Yeh, thanks Dave. Well thankfully that's all they got… "

"Hey, that reminds me, your new phone has arrived, at least that is what it felt like through the Jiffy Bag. I put it in your top drawer. It was in the post box when I arrived yesterday morning. Unlike our IT department to be that quick." Dave said.

"Well, that was quick, I only told Steve to order me a new one at ten o'clock yesterday morning...... When did you say you found this?" Andy said, opening up the sealed padded bag.

"First thing yesterday morning," Dave replied.

Andy removed the phone from the bag and held it; "That's my phone," he said in a surprised tone.

Andy hurriedly switched it on and immediately the text alert sounded, "That'll be Jane, I haven't seen her for ages; that job of hers, they do take liberties."

Andy looked down and saw two texts waiting to be read. Sure enough the first was from Jane, but the second produced an anxious frown - the sender was Eddie. He opened the text and his blood ran cold; it read:

A friendly little warning

that's all Andy

Andy could not believe what he was reading, his headache intensified and he dropped back into his chair. So it wasn't a random mugging after all, and Eddie was behind it. As Andy reflected on the words of the text he certainly understood the warning; but it certainly wasn't little or friendly. The mess he had got himself into was getting deeper by the day.

"Are you okay, Andy?" Dave asked.

"What? Yes, fine," Andy said recovering his senses.

"Jane alright then is she?" Dave said.

"Yeh, fine." Andy said, suddenly realising that he hadn't even opened her text yet. He did so and her words were certainly less intimidating than Eddie's.

Sorry Andy, been sent to Leeds

on a short assignment.

Back Friday xxx

Well, at least that explained Jane's absence. He decided to call her again, now that he at least had got his phone back. He dialled her number but again he went straight to voicemail; "Hi, it's me. Just to let you know that I'm back at work today, I hope you're having fun in Leeds. Call me when you can. Thanks." Andy said, hoping she would call soon; he really was missing her and wanted someone, other than Dave, to speak to.

*

"So what do we do now?" Jez said to his team, who were scattered around their small open plan office. West and Steele were joined by DC Sarah Thompson and DS Tim Warner who had both been members of the OCU for over two years.

"That's what is really odd about this case, Jez," said Sarah Thompson, a petite, attractive brunette whose round face was accentuated by a pageboy style haircut. She was always well groomed and immaculately dressed; unlike many of her counterparts in the force she also took time in the morning to apply makeup. Jez was very fond of her, in a paternal way; she was also a very capable police officer.

The Concrete Grave

"We've spoken to all known informants and nothing. No one knows anything; just like the other cases. Immediately, we've hit a brick wall," she continued.

"What have we learned from the cleaners, Toby?" Jez said turning to the yawning officer, who was downing a large mug of black coffee as he was trying to recover from just four hours sleep.

"I spoke to the cleaner who went into the house. She said that she hadn't seen Sutcliffe for two weeks. But, apparently that is not unusual; even if he's in the house he hides himself away on the top floor and that is out of bounds for the cleaners," Toby explained.

"Interesting. Presumably he does his own vacuuming up there," said Sarah sarcastically. The comment drew a few laughs from her colleagues.

"Well we need to find a lead on this one soon. I'm under pressure from above to get results quickly," Jez said.

"Who reported him missing?" said Tim.

"His wife, Georgina. She seems genuinely in pieces, despite the fact she is likely to inherit a small fortune," Jez replied.

"Is she a suspect, Jez?" Sarah said.

"Yes of course she is. The spouse is always the prime suspect. Didn't you listen to anything they taught you in training? But I do think there is more to this case than a straight forward domestic; and she doesn't seem the type. But we mustn't rule anything out at this stage. Tim, Toby, I want you to cover the airports, check to see if anyone of Sutcliffe's description has been seen there. Rog, you do the same for the ports, Dover, Newhaven etc. We will meet back here this time tomorrow." Jez concluded and turned swiftly towards his office.

"Quick word, Jez?" Sarah said, following him into his small office.

"Sure, Sarah, what's up?"

"Do you think these four killings of gangland heads could be linked?" she said.

"They could well be, yes. Maybe a series of turf wars," Jez replied, "Always happens as a gang starts to flex their muscles and tries to move in on other gangs' territories. But the key to solving this is to find what the link is, and quickly."

"Usually the killers are happy to leak what they've done to increase their strength and superiority, even unofficially. You know, scare off potential threats and the like." Sarah explained carefully.

"Yes, that's true; maybe they've changed tactics, trying to keep everything secret now. Go around to Tommy's old haunts, pubs and clubs etc. and see what you can find out."

"Will do, Jez." Sarah said as she stood and left the office, Lloyd-Brown continued staring at his office door long after she had closed it.

*

The Concrete Grave

As the week progressed Andy's headache lessened, and the last three days of the week went relatively smoothly. The weather was dry, consequently the bricklayers were able to make good progress and they now had over fourteen bricklayers on site to capitalise on the unseasonal sunshine. Friday's QA audit went as well as could be expected, not exceptional, but then again they never were.

However, Andy could not shake off the ever increasing feeling of foreboding. The text he had received from Eddie had shaken him up. One thing was certain, these people were serious, and Andy had every reason to be concerned.

It was Friday though, and as Andy's train pulled in at Petersfield station, the feeling of expectation he had of seeing Jane for the first time in a week was high. As he drove into his short drive he was thrilled to see the lights on and the curtains drawn. As he went to put his key in the lock, the door opened and there was Jane, smiling brightly ready to greet him with a big hug.

"Well, you've been in the wars by the sound of it," she said, "Sit down and tell me all about it."

Jane sat silently and attentively through Andy's long and detailed explanation. At the end she said, "So what are the police doing about it?"

"Nothing, as far as I'm aware. Just one of a hundred muggings in the area every week. I saw nothing and there were no witnesses, so I guess they can't do much."

"Typical, I don't know what the world is coming to. Anyway I bought us a nice steak and an excellent bottle of red wine. I think you need a little TLC this weekend, and I'm going to make sure you get it." With that Jane went into the kitchen and left him sitting on the sofa staring into space with a very guilty conscience.

The steak didn't take long to cook and they both sat down to enjoy the meal. Andy had poured out two large glasses of red wine and as he started to eat Jane took the discussion gently onto the subject of the large outstanding debt.

"Sorry to raise the subject again, Andy, but I've been so worried and I just wanted to clear the air about that dreadful debt I've left us with."

"You need worry about that no longer."

"Why, what's happened?"

"I have received my bonus for my last job, and it's ten thousand pounds. The best thing of all is that I have been paid in cash and therefore I don't have to pay any tax on it." Andy continued.

"What? What do you mean you don't have to pay tax on it? Everything is taxable these days; you can't just accept that sum of cash without declaring it to the taxman," Jane said in a very concerned tone.

"According to the office the taxman is quite happy that certain amounts are paid in that manner providing it is not done too regularly. And considering it's at least two and a half years since I last received a bonus of any sort, that certainly cannot be described as regular," Andy said, hoping his explanation would convince Jane enough to end the debate at that point.

"That's rubbish," said Jane, "You have to pay tax on every penny of income you earn, Andy, trust me. And where have you put the money in the meantime?"

"Well it is safely stored in the back of the wardrobe upstairs. And all I need to do now is to pay into the bank, pay off our debts and our problem is solved."

"One thing's for sure, you will have to produce the paperwork to demonstrate to the bank where you got the money from. The money laundering regulations are very tight nowadays," Jane said in an officious tone. "Presumably you have a remittance slip. It's all about audit trails these days."

"That's the strange thing; there isn't any paperwork with it."

"You'll probably receive something in the post soon."

"Hopefully I will. How was Leeds?" Andy said, trying desperately to change the subject as quickly as possible.

"Quite boring really. As you know I can't tell you too much because of confidentiality. But it was the same old files, full of the same old paperwork, containing the same old numbers. Forensic accounting isn't much fun most of the time."

They finished their meal and Jane said, "I'll tidy up tomorrow, let's have an early night."

Andy was certainly not going to argue as Jane took him by the hand and led him upstairs to the bedroom. Andy was tired, but not that tired.

The Concrete Grave

Chapter Seven

The saloon bar at the Beggars Arms on the Whitechapel Road was dark, dingy and decrepit. But it was the closest drinking facility to the offices of the OCU and its perverseness amused Jeremy Lloyd-Brown.

"So how did it go?" asked Toby as he leant against the dirty, drink-stained, oak bar.

"How did what go?" Jez said as he sipped his whisky and dry ginger ale.

"Your meeting with the Chief Super of course, what else?"

"Oh, that. As bad as you could imagine," Jez replied.

"What did he say?" Toby continued to press for more information which he doubted would be forthcoming.

"He questioned whether we even had a case," Jez said.

"Why?"

"Because, dear boy, there is no body, no witness, no murder weapon and possibly not even a crime."

"How's that?"

"Look at it from his point of view. We have the wife of a gangland thug reporting him missing. We have speculation from the press, who presumably are short of news and have presumed him dead. When all the time I suspect that our old friend Mr Thomas Sutcliffe is laying on a Rio De Janeiro Beach soaking up the sun."

"Is that what you really think?" Toby asked. "That Sutcliffe has done a runner?"

"Yes, I do and I wouldn't be surprised if the press run that story tomorrow."

"How can you be so sure?"

"Because that is the story I leaked to them less than two hours ago."

"Why did you do that?"

"To take the heat off us, that's why. One mention of a London gangster being in Brazil and the dear British public will assume that's the end of that. They have been there before many times, most notably with Ronnie Biggs. It's as good a theory as any. Interest will wane and that'll be it." Jez concluded as he brought his empty whisky glass down on the bar. "Your shout I believe."

Toby called the barman over and ordered another whisky and dry ginger ale and another pint of lager for himself.

"It's strange though isn't it?" Toby mused.

"What's strange?"

"That the *modus operandi* of all four missing gangland heads is the same. Four disappearances, no body found in any instance but a strong suspicion of foul play in each case," Toby said.

"Have you got a better theory?" Jez asked.

"A vigilante group perhaps?"

"An interesting theory, but unlikely."

"Why?" said Toby.

The Concrete Grave

"Well, firstly no vigilante group will be able to get the 'intel'. They couldn't possibly know the workings, structure and leadership of four separate very secretive gangs. Let alone their individual movements at any time of the day. No, it's definitely inter gang rivalry, in a way we haven't seen for several years; even if we assume that they haven't all retired to the Costa Del Sol." Jez said as he finished the last of his whisky. "I'm going back to see how Sarah's getting on. She's reviewing CCTV footage of the area around all Tommy's known haunts over the period shortly before his disappearance. A thankless task, but maybe it will throw up something."

At that Lloyd-Brown turned and left the pub; ignoring the stares he was getting from the locals; his gold tie and Prince of Wales checked suit always stood out in the Beggars Arms. Toby put his half-finished pint on the bar and trotted after him.

*

"How's it going, Sarah?" Jez said as he removed his coat.

"Not the most edifying experience of my life. Three dodgy drug deals; two kerb crawlers and one mugging."

"Only one mugging?" said Jez, "Must've been a quiet week. Anyway keep going, we'll get pilloried if we miss anything."

"How long will we keep on this case?" Sarah asked.

"It ran out of steam almost before it started. A few more days, then we'll be given something else I guess," Jez said as he entered his office. He closed the door behind him just as his mobile phone started to ring.

*

Andy went to work the following Monday with a spring in his step. It had been the best weekend he'd had for some time. Saturday was a wonderful cold sunny day so he and Jane went for a walk around the Devil's Punchbowl, a beauty spot that was just a fifteen minute drive up the A3 trunk road, with wonderful scenery. They followed the walk with a pub lunch and went to the Chinese restaurant in the village for a meal in the evening. Andy used his first fifty pound note from the envelope that Eddie had given him to pay the bill. On Sunday they slept in late, had a long lie in and watched an old film in the afternoon.

The fine weather had continued into Monday as Andy walked along the familiar streets of Tower Hamlets towards the site.

"How's the head?"

Andy turned suddenly as he heard a familiar voice which he couldn't immediately place. When he saw that smile with the familiar gold teeth Andy's feeling of light heartedness changed to grim foreboding in less than a second.

"Eddie, what the hell do you want? Are you stalking me or something?" Andy said in a voice far louder than he had initially intended.

"Calm down; I'm not stalking anyone. I just wanted to see how you were that's all. Just checking that you weren't thinking of doing anything, shall we say, stupid. That's all."

"Look," said Andy, by now genuinely angry, "I'm sick and tired of you and the way you keep harassing me and 'checking up' on me as you so quaintly put it. In fact I think I've had it with you and your criminal ways," Andy was now building up a head of steam, but his fear was increasing, he wondered whether he should just go to the police and come clean. Then this whole wretched mess would be over. But he certainly couldn't let Eddie think he might do that, or the end would come quicker than he would like. "You know what? I'm also fed up waking up at night in a cold sweat or with a lump on my head."

Eddie decided not to pursue the conversation; he turned to go down a side street but, just before he moved out of earshot he turned to Andy and said, "Just don't do anything stupid, that's all," with a strong emphasis on the word 'anything'. At that moment Eddie's mobile phone rang. He took it from his pocket and acknowledged the caller, Andy heard a name but ignored it and continued the short distance to the site, he was angry and scared at the same time and he didn't know what to do. He started his day as usual, with a large mug of coffee.

Eddie turned down the side street and continued his conversation, "Boss, I think we may have a problem. Andy's cracking, could spill his guts."

He listened to the response with a grim expression on his face.

"Yeh, I can handle it. Leave it to me." He finished the call and continued on his way in the general direction of the Canning Town flyover.

*

"We need to get an improvement on the window delivery or we're stuffed," Dave said as he sat with Andy drinking his coffee.

"I'll see what I can do. But, we may have to consider installing temporary protection so we can push on with the plastering."

"We can't afford that, can we?" Dave said.

"You got a better idea?"

"Alright, alright, sorry I spoke. Another bad weekend was it?" Dave said.

"No, as a matter of fact it was a good weekend. It's just Mondays that spoil it," Andy said in a tone which he tried to make as jokey as possible. "How many bricklayers do we have on site today?" Andy said quickly trying to change the subject.

"Fifteen so far, we should be at roof level by Friday."

"Good. Make sure the scaffolders are arranged for Wednesday would you?"

"Already done." Dave said as he turned and grabbed his site helmet before he left the office to check on site labour. He'd decided that it was best to leave Andy alone for a while.

*

"Well, she'll just have to cancel it!" Andy screamed down the phone and he rapidly disconnected the call.

"Who'll have to cancel what?" Dave said, overhearing the final part of the conversation as he entered the office.

Andy sat with his head in his hands. "That bloody architect."

"What, Sylvie?"

"Yes, Sylvie."

"What's she done now?" Dave asked innocently.

"She's only decided to take a skiing holiday at short notice. Just a few days before the final curtain walling details are due."

"You mean the curtain walling details which were due over two weeks ago?"

"Yes, we kindly agreed to a later date and now she's planning on swanning around St Moritz. And if I don't get my curtain walling details for at least another two weeks, the external doors will be late and we won't be able to secure the building. That means the locals around here will help themselves to every length of copper in the building. Some people just haven't got a clue." Andy raged, his day ending as it had begun, with serious aggravation.

"She'll have to cancel it," Dave said.

"Brilliant. I wish I'd thought of that. I was just speaking to her senior partner and told him the same thing.

He doesn't seem to see things the same way as us though. He seems to think that Sylvie needs a break."

"You know your problem?" Dave said, "You get too stressed. Everyone decides to go skiing and you're the only one who worries about the job. Anyway I'm off. I've had enough today."

"Okay. I'll see you tomorrow. I'll stay on and write an appropriately worded e-mail to Mademoiselle Sylvie. Good night, Dave." Andy turned his attention to his laptop and angrily started hammering at the keyboard.

*

Andy arrived home just before nine o'clock. He had worked in the site office far longer than he wanted before he was satisfied with the wording of the email to Sylvie. He pressed send and hoped he wouldn't have any regrets. Steve had always told him to write an email, then sleep on it before reading it again next morning, then send it if you were still happy with the contents. Andy was tired and frustrated, so he pressed 'send'. He felt better immediately.

Once again the house was shrouded in darkness. What's the point of sharing a house with Jane if she's never there? Although he then realised that it was usually him who was late home. Again, it was odd that he hadn't received at least a text from her informing him that she would be late home that evening.

Just as he'd finished drawing the curtains his mobile rang. About time he thought, but it wasn't Jane it was Peter Hill, Andy's oldest and best friend.

"Hi, Pete," said Andy, "How are you doing?"

"Good thanks. I was wondering if you fancy meeting up for a pint tonight?"

"Yeh, sounds like a great idea. It looks like Jane's working late again and I don't fancy another night in on my own. I haven't eaten yet though, so I'll be a while."

"Neither have I. Let's grab something to eat at the White Swan; their steak and ale pies are superb."

"Okay. Sounds great. I'll see you there in about fifteen minutes then?"

The steak and ale pie was indeed delicious as were the two pints that Andy drank with it.

"So how are things with Jane?" Pete asked.

Andy had known Pete since they were at primary school; they had grown up together and had been each other's Best Man at their respective weddings. Pete's marriage had failed around the same time as Andy's and they never hid anything from each other.

"Fine, on the whole. It's just that job of hers; it requires long and unsocial hours. I've hardly seen her at all over the last few weeks." Andy said.

"I thought she was an accountant? Forty hour week and loads of dough," Pete countered.

"Yes, she is, but apparently she has to go to companies at short notice to review their accounts or something like that. You know, if they are being sold. Last week it was Leeds. Who knows where it is this week."

"Why? Hasn't she let you know where she is?" Pete questioned with a suspicious tone.

"No. But before you start, is not what you think."

"How can you be so sure? It's happened before to both of us so, why not again?" said Pete, depressingly reminding them both of the infidelity of their previous partners.

"Oh, thanks for cheering me up. Because we haven't known each other that long; we're still in the honeymoon period. And Jane is not like that."

"Okay, I'll take your word for it. Don't get me wrong, I like her and I think she's good for you too," Pete continued.

"Thanks, and in any case it's usually me who is late home and she should be the one to complain, but she never does," Andy said.

"Last orders." A shout bellowed out across the bar.

"Fancy another?" Pete said.

"Why not? Make it a half as I have an early start in the morning. I'll settle the tab too; I owe you one, or probably two."

"Thanks, Andy," said Pete as he took the crisp new fifty pound note from Andy and headed to the bar to settle up. Pete returned to the table with a pint and a half for Andy.

"Where did you get that fifty pound note from? I haven't seen one of those for ages," Pete said conversationally.

"Mind your own bloody business." Andy said aggressively.

"Sorry for asking. No need to get excited. I wasn't implying that you've just robbed a bank you know."

Andy, suddenly realising that his reaction was not a good idea, quickly moved to cover his tracks.

"Sorry to be jumpy, it's just that I'm not used to carrying that much cash around. I've just received my bonus from my last project."

"What in cash? Who pays bonuses in cash these days?"

"Don't you start. That's what Jane said. It's apparently tax efficient; like salary sacrifice or something."

"You'll have to become an expert in money laundering then. You have to be careful what you do with that amount of cash nowadays or the authorities will be after you. There was a TV programme the other night all about it. Did you see it?"

"What, on money laundering?" Andy was suddenly engaged and showing a lot of interest.

"Yes, it was on Channel 5, came across it when I was channel hopping. Quite interesting actually. It was based on a group of young drug dealers; not about how they got their money, more on what they did with it when they got it."

"Why? What did it say? Tell me."

The Concrete Grave

"Well, basically as long as you are sensible with your ill-gotten gains, you'll be okay."

"I told you, they are not ill-gotten."

"I'm not talking about you, Andy. Don't get so jumpy. Do you want me to tell you or not?"

"Yes please, sorry. Go on."

"Apparently, the way to dispose of that amount of cash is to do it over a period of time and not do anything out of character that would draw attention to you. For example; you could pay for your weekly shop at your local supermarket with the cash. You could pay for your petrol, and some nice meals out could also be bought with cash. How much did you say you had?"

"I didn't. But if you must know it's ten grand."

Pete let out a quiet whistle; "That's quite a bonus. Even so, you could easily use that up within a year or so. You can apparently pay the money into a bank, but that does carry some risk as large amounts of cash would raise suspicions and get reported to the authorities. You can apparently spread it around, different branches or even open several accounts."

"I guess so," Andy said, "Did they give examples of what you can't do?"

"Yes, you wouldn't walk into a Mercedes main dealer with a briefcase containing forty grand to pay for a new C Class for example. That would definitely get reported."

"Fascinating, thanks. We'd better be off, it's getting late."

Andy and Pete finished their drinks, got up from the table and put their coats on. As they headed for the door they turned to the barman and thanked him. As Andy was starting to walk the short distance home, Pete stopped and said, "Are you sure you're okay? You don't seem quite your usual self."

"Yes, I'm fine," Andy replied, "Just tired. Working too hard I guess. See you soon." Andy quickly walked off; he needed his bed. He was also worried about the change in him. He found the discussion on money laundering strangely reassuring but he was feeling down, still worrying about what he had done. He was wondering if he should have told Pete the whole story. He would have only have told him to go to the police though. As he got his keys out to open his front door Andy thought, not for the first time, that that was exactly what he should do, but he knew that would not be a good idea.

*

"Where's Jez?" Toby asked Sarah Thompson.

"I don't know. Out I expect, as usual."

"He's always out. What does he get up to? Most DCI's I've worked with in the past spend their entire time in front of a computer screen writing reports. Jez never seems to write any."

"He's probably meeting his financial adviser to discuss his stocks and shares. He's got more money than the entire team will ever have. Can't understand why he does this job. Doesn't really make sense to me. I'm not complaining though; best boss I've had since I joined the force."

"Me too. He's a good bloke and you can't say that about many DCI's these days. I guess he likes running a small team. He has plenty of autonomy, that's for sure," Toby said.

"Yes, he certainly has. Don't know how he gets away with it really, what did you want him for anyway?" Sarah said.

"It's this Tommy Sutcliffe case; it's going nowhere and I'm fed up with running into brick walls all the time."

"Yes it's odd. I have not come up with anything either. Not a single solitary lead have we got between us," Sarah said.

At that moment the door opened. Jez walked in with his mobile phone held against his ear. "You'll just have to sort it out yourself. You got into the mess, now get yourself out of it." He angrily rang off and thrust his phone into its pocket.

"Who was that?" Toby said.

"None of your business," Jez said, and then suddenly correcting himself he changed tone completely and continued, "It was the wife; bought herself a new four by four to take Sophie to school in and it won't fit in the garage. Can you believe that? It's not as if our garage is small, it's not. The car she bought is huge; we'll have to get the builders in now to increase the size of the garage."

"Typical," said Toby, "They never think these things through do they? I'm glad you walked in boss, I wanted a word with you about the case."

"We press on until we are told otherwise. We're police officers and that is what policing is all about; discipline and rigour. We must make completely sure that we leave no stone unturned. Sorry if that offends, but that's the rules," Jez said.

"Okay. I understand. I'll go back to his house in the morning I think, and see if I can find anything more there. There must be some clues there somewhere. Perhaps I'll even find a body."

"Now that would be helpful." Jez replied.

West left the office after receiving the answer he didn't want and Jez went towards his office door, stopped and looked at his watch, turned on his heel and followed West out through the door and towards the street.

*

The black cab pulled into the kerb outside the RAC Club. Pall Mall was busy, it was almost eight o'clock and people were either heading home after work, or going to a restaurant or the theatre.

Jez gave the cabbie a ten pound note, "Keep the change."

"Thanks, mate," replied the cabbie as he pulled back into the busy traffic in search of his next fare.

Most police officers, if they were honest, would admit to feeling uncomfortable in an establishment like the RAC Club. But not Jeremy Lloyd-Brown, with his handmade suit and tailored shirt with co-ordinating silk tie he looked very much at home in these surroundings.

The Concrete Grave

He walked across the grand marble foyer, passing the silver Aston Martin DB5 parked at the bottom of the main stairs. It was in pristine condition and Jez gave it a covetous glance as he made his way up the carpeted staircase towards the usual meeting room.

The large portraits on the dark wood panelled walls stared down at him as he ascended the stairs. He loved this place, it gave him a buzz every time he went there.

He walked along a wide corridor and looked at paintings of Bluebird and the classic E Type Jaguar. He stopped at a large panelled door, opened it slowly and entered a medium-sized room which had a table large enough to seat about twelve people, although there would be not that many there tonight.

"Hey, Jez, come over here," a large smartly dressed man with a full mop of dark hair was calling to him from the far side of the room, he beckoned him towards him and the person he was speaking to.

"Hello, Colin," Jez said, shaking his hand in a firm and friendly manner.

"Jez, you know Alastair don't you?"

"Yes of course, how are you, Alistair?" The two exchanged handshakes.

"I'm fine thanks, although listening to Colin's anecdotes at this time of day can be a little tiresome."

"A large G&T over here please," Colin said beckoning to the smartly dressed waiter holding a silver tray.

"Jez, I was just telling Alastair about that double hundred you made at Fenners, the best innings I have ever seen."

"Now, Colin, you're exaggerating, but we were playing St John's. They certainly weren't expecting to be beaten by little Downing. Having said that, batting conditions were perfect."

"Do you still play, Jez?" Alastair asked.

"No time in my job," Jez said with a laugh, "I would like to play more though."

"He could have made the grade at county standard, no problem. What with his batting and my spin bowling Downing won everything for three years. Do you remember that party after your double century, Jez?"

"Not much of it no. Other than you jumping off that bridge into the River Cam," Alistair laughed politely.

"We broke the record for the most bottles of champagne purchased in one night at the students' bar. Those were the days."

"Time to stop reminiscing now, Colin," said a very tall grey haired man who had crept up on them unheard, "We have business to do."

The seven smartly dressed men sat around one end of the long table. The grey haired man sat at the head and took control.

"Now, we have all the stakeholders present, Jez would you like to give us an update on progress so far?"

"Certainly, Gerald," said Jez as he looked down at the blank notepad in front of him and started to give his report.

Chapter Eight

Andy's alarm clock buzzed on at five o'clock as usual. His mouth was dry and his head ached, despite the fact that he had only drunk two and a half pints last night. He put his left arm across the bed and felt that Jane still hadn't got back. He wondered where she was, pondering on the insinuations that Pete had made last night.

He quickly got out of bed and had a shower. Today was going to be busy and stressful. It was the day of the monthly client meeting when he had to report on progress. Steve would be there, but so would the dreaded Sonia Clark, head of the Borough's schools' building programme, a powerful woman in more ways than one. She did not like the thought of any of her schools being completed late, so Andy had to come up with a way of convincing her that St Oswald's would finish on time, despite currently being over four weeks behind programme. Andy considered his tactics as he looked out of the train window, the dark Hampshire countryside passing by in a seemingly endless blur.

He was, however, giving more thought to what he was going to do next to resolve the recent events which had left him continually depressed and deeply worried. He was involved in something much deeper than he could possibly have imagined. His life, and probably Jane's, were now in extreme danger. He was involved with a gang who had just disposed of a high profile gangster, surely they would not think twice about killing him. He could possibly speak to Steve but, although he trusted him, he may feel obliged to tell Norman and then things would get complicated. The real pressure he felt was not having anyone to speak to about the situation he found himself in.

As Andy walked across the concourse of Waterloo station he felt the weight of the world on his shoulders. He was usually so laid back, but this was really getting to him. His thoughts turned to today's client meeting, he needed something else to think about.

He entered site slightly earlier than usual and, just as he was starting to climb the stairs, the text alert on his mobile sounded. He waited until he was in the office, took his coat off and sat down. He took out his phone, fully expecting the text to be from Jane giving him an apologetic update on her current whereabouts. He opened the text, his assumption was partly correct, it did give him an update on Jane's whereabouts, but not in the manner he had expected. The text was from Eddie:

> Don't worry about Jane.
>
> She's in safe hands.
>
> Just don't do anything stupid.
>
> Eddie

Andy read the text twice and felt physically sick; he stared blankly at the wall opposite unable to think straight.

"You okay, Andy?" Dave said as he entered the office. "Looks like you've seen a ghost. Worried about today's meeting?"

"No, eerrr yes, I'm fine thanks, just thinking through the best way to explain how we're going to recover the four weeks lost time in the second half of the project," Andy replied.

"We're not gonna be able to are we?" Dave said.

"No, of course were not, but I can't tell them that, can I?" Andy said.

"What are you going to say then?" Dave continued.

"That we're in the process of drawing up a recovery programme, which will compress the critical path items to achieve the required completion date."

"Sounds impressive to me."

"It's *bullshit,* Dave; that's what it is. But it should be enough to keep the pressure off for another month."

At that moment Steve walked into the office.

"Morning, how are we all?" he asked cheerily.

Andy and Dave both looked at Steve blankly.

"Not so good by the look of it," Steve said.

"We're just working out the best way to tell the client that they will get their school on time without making it looked like an enormous lie." Andy said.

"Now that's a tricky one," Steve said. "Not expecting an easy meeting then?"

"No we're not, and if Mrs Sonia-bossy-boots-Clark starts to get heavy, I may well be tempted to insert my site helmet where the sun doesn't shine." Andy exploded.

"Woa, steady now, I'm not sure how we'd explain that entry in the accident book. Perhaps, Andy, we'll just have to tell the truth. We've got some good reasons for the delay, some of which we might get paid for," Steve said, attempting to calm the situation knowing that the client may walk through the door at any moment.

"Not under this contract we won't, even if we break wind it costs us money. I'm not sure who agreed to sign such an onerous agreement," Andy said.

"Anyway, we'd best not go there, let's have a quick look round the job before we start," Steve said and, after they had both kitted themselves out with safety equipment, they left the office.

As they walked round the far end of the building Steve turned to Andy and said, "What is wrong, Andy? I have known you for almost twenty years and I have never known you like this before. Something's up; would you like to talk about it?"

"Not really," Andy said sullenly.

"What are you doing after work tonight? Fancy a drink and a bite to eat?"

Andy's mind raced, he was hoping that he might see Jane tonight but, following the receipt of the text that wasn't going to happen. The idea of a free meal and some company sounded more appealing than it might have done on other occasions.

"Yes, okay. Sounds like a good idea. Things aren't great at home at the moment and it'll give me a chance to talk things through," Andy said.

"Good, I'm sure we can find somewhere suitable locally."

Andy was not so sure, but didn't say anything as they headed back to the site office.

If anything, the client meeting went worse than Andy had expected. They had decided to follow Steve's strategy of telling the truth, but it wasn't well received. Sonia Clark was on top form, taking the best part of fifteen minutes to tell everyone in the room that the mere thought that her school would complete late was totally unacceptable and if necessary she'd find another contractor who would complete the work on time.

I wish she would, Andy thought as he sat at the top of the table with his head in his hands. But, in the circumstances, he decided not to say anything as he knew that it would only compound the problem.

The meeting ended with Sonia Clarke announcing that she would contact Chapples Chief Executive, Norman Doyle as soon as she got back to her office. No doubt he'd sort things out. She left the office slamming the door, her ample frame shaking the external stairs as she departed in some haste.

*

"Has Norman had his call yet?" Andy said as he scanned the menu. They were sitting in comfortable leather chairs in a surprisingly upmarket steakhouse, not far from the site, that Andy hadn't noticed before.

"Oh yes," replied Steve, "fortunately I warned him that it was coming and gave him an update on the current situation. Sirloin steak sounds good. Fancy a glass of red wine with it? I think we'll order a bottle after the day's events."

"Red wine would be great and I'll have the sirloin steak too, with hollandaise sauce I think."

Steve gave their order to the friendly waitress who quickly returned with the bottle of the selected Rioja and poured a little into his glass. He tasted it, gave a discerning nod of approval and she filled both glasses.

"Did that discussion with Norman help matters?" Andy said, taking a large gulp of the wine.

"A little. He hates being hijacked by a client, especially one like Sonia Clark. He was okay but, as you'd probably expect, he's clearing his diary one day next week to personally undertake a thorough review of the project."

"Oh no, I know what that means."

"Yes, we'll all waste a lot of time compiling reports detailing programme position, forecasting the margin secured on orders placed, then another one for orders not placed, together with a full breakdown of our preliminaries."

"Only to be told that it is 'unacceptable' or; if he's in really bad mood, 'totally unacceptable.'"

"You said that, not me. But you're right, Norman will want a daily report and he'll want to validate all decisions, which will delay things further and the left hand won't know what the right hand is doing."

"So how long will this go on for?" Andy asked.

"Usually about two weeks, then there will be a bigger crisis on another project. The focus of attention will turn to that, allowing us to get on with our job."

"You're being a bit cynical aren't you?"

"That's reality, Andy. We'll call in the managing directors of the sub-contractors, we know them well enough. We'll explain our position and ask them for help. They'll pull out the stops for us. They always do. It may cost us a bit, but they'll get the project over the line. One piece of good news though."

"Oh, what's that? I could certainly use some."

"When I spoke to Norman I took the opportunity to tell him that we needed an extra foreman."

"I thought we couldn't afford one."

"We can't, but I told him that it would be a false economy not to have one. He agreed that we should draft someone else in."

"That is good news. Is Tim Smith free? He'd be great for this job." Andy said.

"I'll see what I can do."

Their steaks arrived and, as they started eating, Steve changed the subject from work to Andy's personal life.

"Problems at home, you said. Anything serious?"

"Hopefully not. It's a combination of our jobs. Frankly, we don't see much of each other. We're like ships that pass in the night. Her job at the moment seems more onerous than mine. Last week she had to go to Leeds at short notice. This week she's………." Andy quickly stopped, remembering that he now knew exactly the predicament Jane was in and did not have a clue how to deal with it.

"She's where, Andy?" Steve said, as Andy failed to finish his sentence.

"That's just it, I don't really know, she may have told me but I haven't heard from her since Sunday night. This steak's good though."

"She's probably very busy and totally focused on the job in hand. We all make the mistake of putting our loved ones second to the job at times. Why don't you take some time off? Use your bonus to find some early winter sunshine. I've heard that Portugal is still quite warm this time of year."

"Steve, I haven't received any bonus yet and you know full well that I can't leave Dave to run the job at this stage. The thought is appealing though, I must admit."

"The letter advising you of the bonus will be sent out on Friday and I'll arrange for Simon Reed to sit in for you. He's the best I've got. He could review things for you too," Steve helpfully added.

"Yes, Simon's good, I'll think about it, could be helpful."

The truth was that Andy would like to take some time off, not to go to Portugal but to attempt to find out what Eddie had done with Jane, but he had no idea where to start looking.

Steve ordered another bottle of wine and they finished their meal talking about football, which took Andy's mind off things. Steve was an avid Spurs supporter and they were playing Liverpool on Sunday, so they passed a good half hour discussing each other's chances.

Andy thanked Steve as they left the restaurant and they set off in opposite directions. The wine had made Andy feel light headed, but had done nothing to quell the feelings of anger and frustration which were building up inside him. The restaurant was situated slightly off Andy's normal route but he thought he'd find his way back to Canning Town tube station, even if he hadn't walked that route before. It was almost ten o'clock; the streets were dark and far from inviting. Andy set off at a fast pace; the less time he spent in this part of London at this time of night the better he thought.

His sense of direction had always been quite good and he was confident that he was heading east in the general direction of the tube station. He turned right into a narrow road with decaying three storey Victorian houses on either side, the rusty street sign told him that the road was called Shackleton Road. The street lighting gave off a soft but irregular light and Andy couldn't help noticing the odd assortment of vehicles that were parked on both sides of the road. Some looked as though they had been parked there for years. Andy hurried along the dimly lit street, there were a few people just loitering around in groups of twos and threes on street corners. Andy was pleased that they weren't larger in number. As he walked along he wasn't aware that he was looking at anything specific, but his subconscious mind alerted him to something and he stopped dead. Parked on the side of the road was a white transit van. It wasn't that alone that caused him to stop; it was the last three letters on the registration plate of this particular van, GON. He recalled the irony of Eddie's comment; 'Gone by lunchtime', and he was. He took a closer look at the van, the rear wheel arches were muddy and he was in no doubt that this was the van used by Eddie and his men to deliver the body of Tommy Sutcliffe to site that fateful night.

The Concrete Grave

Andy was not sure what to do. Frankly he wasn't particularly bothered where Eddie or any of his men lived, it was of no importance to him. Or was it? Maybe this knowledge could give him a slight edge. Andy stood in the dark shadow of the van looking at the adjacent row of terraced houses. Two of the four had ground floor lights on, and the one dead opposite the van had partly drawn curtains. Curiosity got the better of Andy and he crept up the short path leading to the metal plated front door. He stepped off the path and ducked under the window sill, his mind in turmoil. Part of his brain was calling him an idiot and a fool, questioning his actions. The other part was encouraging him to take a look inside and see if he could identify any of the miscreants from the early hours of Friday morning. Was it really less than two weeks ago?

As he crouched down beneath the crumbling concrete window sill he heard raised voices. Two men were clearly arguing, he thought he recognised one of the voices but he wasn't sure. He cautiously poked his head above the window sill and saw the two men. One was sitting in an armchair which had its back to the window; the other was standing in the hallway with what looked like a bottle of beer in his hand. This man was looking at the man in the armchair but the direction he was looking made it look as though he was looking towards Andy, through the gap in the curtains. Andy ducked, concerned that he'd been seen, although from the reaction of the men inside the house, there was no indication that he had been. As the men calmed down, the anger in their voices abating, he heard the man in the door say, "I don't care, you do it your way," as he walked out of sight. The seated man kept talking though in a tone that indicated that there was someone else in the room. Andy tried to crane his neck in the general direction that the seated man appeared to be looking, but he couldn't see anything else from the angle he was positioned.

Then he heard a voice, it was that of a woman, and a voice he knew well. It couldn't be. He changed position, pressed his head tighter against the wall and then he could just see the profile of a blonde haired woman. The hair was different but there was no doubt from the profile that it was Jane. Andy stopped breathing; he closed his eyes, he must be dreaming. What on earth could Jane be doing in a rundown town house so close to the construction site where he worked? The wine must've slowed his thought process for it was only then that Andy realised that this is where Eddie and his cronies had taken her after she had been kidnapped.

As Andy continued to look through the gap in the curtains he could see that Jane was sitting in an adjacent armchair looking extremely uncomfortable, she was talking to the other man reluctantly in a stressed tone. It looked as though she was tied to the chair with her arms behind her, held together at the wrists, but from the position Andy was in he couldn't be certain.

Andy looked back at the street and realised that if anyone came to visit the house, or even walk past, he would be a sitting duck. The backs of his thighs were starting to ache due to the crouching position he had been in, so he gingerly stood up and made his way back to the street. He slowly walked along a pavement in the direction he had been heading previously, but Andy had forgotten all about heading back to the tube station now. The anger inside him was now close to bursting point; his inclination was to rush in and make an heroic rescue, but he knew that he needed time to take stock of the situation. About fifty yards further along the road there was a pub, with noise blaring and the sound of raised voices. He needed somewhere to go to sit and think and, as it had just started to drizzle, that seemed as good a place as any to go.

As Andy entered the pub, The Carpenter's Arms, he almost changed his mind. He had thought the Prince of Wales, the pub where he first met Eddie was rough, but that was like the Palm Court at the Ritz compared to the sight in front of him. He had heard stories of pubs with sawdust on the floor to allow the clientele to spit at will and to facilitate easy cleaning, but he'd never seen one in the flesh, until now. The pub was heaving too, frequented by every kind of low life imaginable. He warily made his way to the bar.

The barman was a skinny, hunched, crooked-shouldered man in a moth-eaten, ill-fitting pullover. His greasy brown hair and beard obscured most of his face, except the eyes that stared out in a way that was reminiscent of the photographs you see of mass murderers that often make the front pages of our daily newspapers. "Yes mate, what do you want?" he said in an unfriendly manner. Andy was uncertain whether it was a request for his order or a threat. He took the easy option and assumed that it was the former.

"A pint of lager please," Andy said.

"Please?" the barman said mockingly. "I remember that word, last heard it spoken in here about five years ago."

Andy decided to say nothing and took his drink, paying the barman in change. He decided against saying thank you, realising he'd drawn too much attention to himself already. He was surprised to see an empty corner table and headed for that. As he approached it, a large hand appeared and landed on the table with a loud thump.

"I wouldn't sit there if I was you," said a gruff voice. "Charlie's in the bog, he'll be back in a minute." Andy wasn't minded to argue and backed off.

"You can sit here if you want," the man continued pointing to the empty seat at his table, a very small table. There were no other obvious seats and Andy wanted to sit down. Also, it would have seemed rude to refuse the offer, and apparent rudeness in an establishment like this one would have been equivalent to an invitation for a fight. So Andy nodded his thanks and sat on the empty seat, putting his pint of lager on the small soiled table.

He sipped his drink and started thinking through what he had just seen, considering his options.

"You're not from round here are you?" The question came from the man sitting next to Andy at the table. He spoke without even looking at him.

"No, not really, I work not far from here though," replied Andy, being as polite as he could.

"Work? Around here? Aren't you the lucky one?" the man said sarcastically.

Andy decided not to enter into conversation with someone who clearly was not the friendliest of individuals. His unshaven face and the scruffy overcoat merely giving support to Andy's concerns. A few minutes passed and Andy's mind returned to the issue at hand and exactly what his next step should be. His sensible side told him to note the address and go straight to the police. But what if Jane got hurt in the resulting raid? He'd heard a number of stories of police raids in the area and the heavy handed tactics involved. Kick the door in, shoot first and ask questions later seemed to be the *modus operandi* in these parts; and who could blame the police for employing those tactics when you considered the average calibre of the local populous.

"What yer do?" the gruff voice said. It had been fully five minutes since the man had last spoken and Andy had noticed that his focus had not moved from the blank wall opposite. Andy was slow to reply. "I said, what you do?" the man repeated in a distinctly more aggressive tone than the first question.

"I'm a project manager," Andy said quickly, "I work on the construction site at St Oswald's School," hoping that his response would give him another five minutes respite; but he was wrong.

"I went there," the man said.

"Where?" Andy said slightly confused.

"St Oswald's School. That was a long time ago mind, it was a good school then. Not like now, kids have it too soft now they do," the man continued.

"Yes, I suppose they do," agreed Andy, hoping to keep the conversation to a minimum. The previous silence resumed and Andy went back to exploring his options, not for the first time in the past two weeks, he decided that they were seriously limited.

His only other obvious option was to somehow get into the house and help Jane to escape. She was clearly in some discomfort and had changed, not just her demeanour but her appearance as well. Andy couldn't work out what was going on.

"Ever since they stopped caning the little blighters the world's gone to pot. Never did me any harm," the man blurted. Andy felt minded to voice his disagreement to that last sentence, but thought better of it. The steak meal he'd had with Steve barely two hours ago seemed but a distant memory.

Andy finished his lager and stood up to leave. "Nice meeting you," lied Andy, just hearing the grunt as he walked towards the door, a plan now firmly fixed in his mind.

He walked swiftly back towards the house along the opposite side of the road, his anger had reached breaking point, not a good emotional state to be in, but at least anger would sustain him and help him to do what he had to do. When he was directly opposite he stepped back and thought. He needed a weapon and as he looked around him he saw just what he was looking for. A short length of scaffold tube was lying in the road against the kerb. Andy had no idea what it was doing there but it couldn't have been better placed for him. He picked it up and knew he had to act quickly. He jogged across the road, concealing the metre long piece of tube by his side as best he could.

He reached the rusty steel-faced front door and pressed the door bell, uncertain whether it was working or not.

After a short while, which seemed like an eternity to Andy, he heard the heavy door being unlocked more than once and he pressed his back as hard as he could against the wall of the house adjacent to the front door. The door slowly opened and light flooded onto the small stone step illuminating the excuse for a front garden which was festooned with rubbish. Andy waited, daring not to breath. He wanted the man to step outside to see who had rung the bell.

"Are you sure you heard the bell, Tone?" a voice said.

"Yeah, who is it?" the other man replied.

At that the man moved forward onto the step, it was now or never. With any fear he might have felt negated by a bottle of Rioja, Andy slowly lifted the length of scaffold tube up until it was parallel to the ground and releasing all his pent up anger he swung it in an anticlockwise arc as hard as he could into the man's midriff. The man let out a stifled gasp as he doubled up and immediately Andy pulled the tube back. He lifted it into the air as if he was a lumberjack chopping a large log and brought it down squarely onto the back of the exposed neck of the man. Time seemed to stand still. Then, slowly and silently the man keeled over forwards into a heap on to the path. Andy stood looking at his handiwork, shocked by the effectiveness of it. A voice from inside the house shook him back to reality.

"Who was it, Taff?"

Andy quickly entered the front door and realised that the voice was coming from the rear of the house at ground floor level, presumably the kitchen. Uncertain of what to do next, he stood silently in the hall at the bottom of the stairs. Then he heard a sound coming from upstairs, one he immediately recognised, it was a cough, and it was unmistakably Jane's familiar cough. His instincts took over, he closed the front door silently and gingerly started to climb the stairs, every small creak and squeak seemingly being amplified a thousand times. He reached the top of the stairs, his blood pounding in his ears. He turned left around the banisters towards a door which was slightly open. He stopped and listened outside the door for a few moments. Nothing. He poked his head round the door and, from the mottled light that shone from the street light outside through the shabby lace curtains, he saw someone lying on her side on the bed, apparently bound at wrists and ankles. He knew it was Jane, but she looked very different, as if she'd had an extreme reverse makeover. Her hair looked greasy and tied back with an elastic band as Andy had never seen it before. She had what looked like a tattoo of a spider's web on her neck, as well as piercings through her nose and upper lip. Andy took a closer look, it was definitely Jane and she was either dozing or drugged. He was uncertain which and he quickly knelt at the side of the bed facing Jane and gently shook her.

"Jane, wake up, it's me."

"Whaaat?" Jane said, as she slowly opened her eyes. A look of shock passed across her face as she realised who it was kneeling in front of her.

"Andy, what on earth? How did you get here?"

"I might ask you the same thing," Andy replied. "No time for questions. Let's get out of here." Andy quickly untied Jane's ankles and started to untie the rope that bound her wrists, but was stopped short by the sound of a voice behind him.

The Concrete Grave

"You're not going anywhere you toe rag, that's for sure," said a voice belonging to a very large man standing in the doorway holding what, in the half light, looked to Andy remarkably like a gun. He froze, having never seen a real gun before and just stared at the man with his mouth open. What happened next took him completely by surprise. Jane, who had managed to free herself from the rope around her wrists, leapt forward and, with both hands, grabbed the top rail of the metal bedstead at the foot of the bed. Then, with the dexterity of an Olympic gymnast, she swung her body over the rail catching the large, armed man fully in the face with both feet. The man staggered backwards dropping the gun onto the floor. Jane's acrobatic manoeuvre left her on the floor but she was swiftly on to her feet planting a well-aimed karate kick into the man's solar plexus. Unfortunately for Jane the man was quicker than she thought and he grabbed her foot as it found its target and pushed her backwards into the bedroom.

"The gun, Andy," Jane shouted, "Get that gun!"

But Andy was too slow. A large foot appeared from outside of the room and stood on the revolver. Andy looked up, the foot belonged to a man who looked remarkably like the one he had pole-axed minutes earlier with the scaffold tube. He'd only seen the man in silhouette in the door frame but he was certain it was him and the next words rather confirmed the fact.

"Think you're hard do you? I'll show you hard," he grunted.

By now Jane seemed to be on top in her fight with the first man. He was face down on the floor and Jane had both her knees in his back and her right arm fully around his windpipe. Andy realised he had no time to watch Jane, even though she was behaving in a way that was totally alien to him. He looked up, slowly got up from his knees and, without really thinking, launched himself headfirst towards the man who was standing in the door opening. Andy's bulk and strong legs gave him unexpected power and velocity as the top of his head met with the man's midriff, for a second time the man was caught completely off guard by Andy. The large man struggled as he tried to stop himself being knocked over and took a couple of steps backwards, through the door opening and onto the landing. There was a loud crack as his back hit the banister rail behind him. The rail snapped as if it was made of balsa wood and the man fell backwards, headfirst, hitting the stairs below with a sickening thud. Andy's momentum carried him close to the newly exposed edge and he just managed to grab a post from the broken bannister with his right hand, which stopped him just in time. He looked down to see the lifeless body which this time didn't look as though it was about to repeat its earlier resurrection.

Andy went back into the bedroom to find Jane standing up and brushing her hands together in a manner that said; job done. The other man also lay motionless on the floor.

"Have you……killed him?" spluttered a puzzled Andy, who had a million other questions running through his brain at the time.

"I could ask you the same thing," said Jane as she grabbed Andy's arm and ran towards the top of the stairs. "There's no time for answers now, let's get out of here."

They clambered over the stricken body, down the stairs to the front door, which was still ajar and ran down the path to the street. They stopped by the white Ford Transit van that Andy had identified earlier in the evening.

"We need to get away from here, and quickly," Andy said.

Jane held up her right hand which was holding a set of car keys. She quickly unlocked the driver's door, opened it and jumped into the driver's seat starting the engine seemingly all in one single motion. Andy stood rooted to the spot, mouth open, unable to quite believe what he was watching.

"Well, are you going to get in or stand there like a stuffed dummy?" Jane said.

Andy quickly ran round the rear of the vehicle and got into the passenger seat, barely having time to close the door before Jane had gunned the accelerator and headed away from the scene of devastation at top speed.

"Where on earth did you learn to do that?" said Andy, once he had belted himself in and placed his hands by his thighs, gripping the edges of the seat very tightly.

"Learn to do what?" Jane replied.

"To fight like thaaaat – whoooa watch it." said Andy as Jane deftly flicked out the rear end of the van on the greasy road surface. She took a left hand turn at double the speed that Andy would normally consider safe, and he didn't regard himself as a slow driver.

"Just hang on tight and keep an eye behind us," Jane said.

The Concrete Grave

Andy decided that the best thing was to obey. Jane was hurling the white van through the side streets of Tower Hamlets with all the panache of Jeremy Clarkson at his best. Andy kept an eye on the wing mirror to his left and suddenly saw an intermittent blue flash which could only mean one thing.

"Police car to the stern," said Andy "At last, sanctuary. We can now come clean and be safe from these thugs." Although Andy wasn't sure just how 'clean' he would come.

Jane carefully slowed down and pulled the van into the kerb. She wound down the passenger window as a policeman got out from the car that was now parked in front of her nose in to the kerb.

"In a hurry are we miss?" he said somewhat sarcastically.

"Not really, we just needed to escape from a nasty little incident," said Jane. Andy was amazed at her total nonchalance, as he realised he was shaking like a leaf.

"Please get out and move to the rear of the vehicle," said the policeman far more politely than Andy felt he should have been.

Andy and Jane moved to the back of the van as the other officer in the passenger seat of the police car joined them.

"Arms on the rear doors and feet wide apart please," the first policeman said. "What?" Andy said, "We're not the criminals you know."

"Just do it, Andy, it doesn't help to argue. They're just doing their job," Jane ordered.

"Thank you," the police officer replied, maintaining an artificially polite tone.

Just then Andy saw on the ground between his open legs the headlights of another car parking against the kerb behind them. The front of the car getting rather too close to the backs of his legs for comfort he thought. He heard a car door open and slam shut. This was followed by the sound of another three car doors being slammed shut.

"Thanks boys. We'll take it from here," said a gruff voice that sounded vaguely familiar. "Hands behind your back." Andy felt his hands being pulled roughly together at the wrists and tied by what felt like plastic cable ties.

The two policemen silently returned to their car, turned off the blue flashing light and slowly drove away.

"Where the hell are they going?" Andy gasped.

"Shut it and turn around," said the voice.

Andy and Jane both did as they were told. Clearly they were in no position to argue.

Andy had thought that he'd had more than enough bad news for one night, but he was wrong. He looked at the unmistakable gold teeth in the mouth of the smiling face which could only belong to one person. Eddie McNerney.

The Concrete Grave

Chapter Nine

Although it was late, Sarah Thompson and Toby West were still working, determined to get a breakthrough in the case. The office was dark and dingy and not a great place to be. Sarah was working through more CCTV footage and West had just returned from another visit to Sutcliffe's house.

"So, did you find anything more?" Sarah said.

"Nothing, absolutely nothing. No paperwork, no diary, no computer. Nothing. It's all really odd," Toby replied.

"Perhaps that gives credence to Jez's theory that he's done a runner to Brazil or somewhere."

"Yes, I guess so. It's what they teach in training - the perfect murder is one where there is no body, and in this case possibly not even a victim."

Toby's reflections were interrupted by the phone ringing. Sarah picked it up.

"D S Thompson," she said as she listened attentively to the caller. "Yes," she said several times growing in enthusiasm. "Yes, that is very helpful." She hurriedly took down some details. "Thank you." She concluded the call and replaced the receiver. She sat back in a chair and raised both arms towards the ceiling emitting a loud triumphant shout.

"Yes. A breakthrough at last."

"Who was that?" Toby questioned.

"That was Hayes and Harlington CID. Some very thorough individual was running through some crime reports when he saw our missing person report related to Tommy

Sutcliffe. They realised that the timings were close to a report they had on their patch of a scuffle which ended apparently with a man being bundled into a van. He compared the descriptions and it appears that we may have a match."

"Hayes and Harlington, what on earth would Sutcliffe be doing in that part of London?" Toby said.

"I don't know, but it is the very first lead we've had on this case and I intend following it up right now."

"Now? Isn't a little late for that?"

Sarah looked at her watch, "Yes I guess it is – it'll wait until tomorrow. If we can get some CCTV footage taken at the time of the incident and it turns out to be Sutcliffe, we may be able to ID the vehicle or maybe even the perpetrators."

"What's all the excitement?" Jez Lloyd-Brown had walked in unnoticed behind Sarah.

"Hi, Jez. We've got a possible breakthrough at last in the Sutcliffe case," Sarah told him as she turned round.

"That's rather unfortunate timing," Jez said.

"Why? What?"

"I've just received a call from the Chief and we are to drop the Sutcliffe case forthwith. According to him we've already wasted too much time and money on what in all probability is a wild goose chase," Jez informed them both.

"It might not be now," Sarah said.

"Why? What's happened to change things?"

Sarah explained the call she had received from Hayes and Harlington CID and assured Jez that she'd follow it up first thing in the morning.

"You won't be following anything up related to the Sutcliffe case; it's closed."

"Who says so?" Sarah responded angrily.

"The Chief does and so do I, and that's good enough for you." Jez replied, "Anyway we now have other fish to fry. We are receiving reports of increased extortion and prostitution in the Islington area. We're to find out what's going on and discover who is becoming active there," Jez said.

"We can't drop the Sutcliffe case now, Jez, not just as we've got our first break," Sarah said defiantly.

"Yes we can and we will, or you'll have me to answer to. Islington it is for you two from first thing tomorrow. Now go home, get some rest and report back here at eight o'clock tomorrow morning for a briefing." Jez turned and went into his office, closing the door behind him.

"We can't stop now, it would be criminal if we didn't follow up this lead. It was only the other day when he was lecturing us about not leaving any stone unturned," Sarah continued.

"You heard the boss. Our job is not to reason why, just do what we're told. I'm off as instructed. Goodnight." Toby got up, grabbed his coat and walked to the door, he quickly turned round and looked back at Sarah, "See you tomorrow."

By then Sarah had her head in her hands which she had clenched into tight fists around her hair. She was fuming and confused. The question was, what would she do next?

Within a few minutes she'd made up her mind. The briefing for the new Islington job may well be at eight o'clock tomorrow morning, but there was plenty of time between then and now to do something productive, and no one ever need know.

She got up, grabbed her coat and left the office. She went round the corner to the enclosed area behind the police station where the pool cars were kept. She signed out a car, which she was quite entitled to do, and she drove west.

She decided to drive through the centre of London, it was almost midnight and the roads were quiet enough to make this the quickest route. There was also another reason; Sarah thoroughly enjoyed driving through London at night and, despite the fact that it was only just December, the Christmas lights were up and they made the capital look even more colourful than it normally did.

The journey was just over twenty miles and it took almost an hour. She found the police station at Hayes with ease and parked adjacent to the main entrance.

Sarah approached the front door and showed her warrant card.

"DS Thompson for DC Worsfold, he is expecting me," she said.

The young uniformed constable behind the desk smiled at Sarah, picked up the phone and dialled an extension.

While he was waiting for an answer he asked conversationally, "Where have you travelled from?"

"Tower Hamlets," Sarah said, determined not to enter into a conversation.

"Ian, a D S Thompson here to see you," he listened to the response and replaced the receiver.

"He'll be right down. Must be urgent?" he added turning to Sarah.

"Why must it?" Sarah replied in a more confrontational tone than she'd wanted.

"Considering where you've come from and the time of day I meant," the constable added attempting to justify his initial comment.

"I've always considered working in the police force to be a vocation not a job," Sarah said somewhat pompously. "If something needs doing then it has to be done."

The constable was relieved from his embarrassment by the voice of a man coming through the security door by the front desk.

"D S Thompson? DC Worsfold, good to meet you," he held out his right hand and Sarah shook it warmly. "Would you like to follow me?" he said.

The young DC led Sarah down a plain corridor and into a small room which more often than not would be used as an interview room.

"May I get you a coffee?" DC Worsfold asked.

"Thanks that would be good."

"Machine only I'm afraid."

"That's fine."

He was gone only a couple of minutes and returned with two plastic cups full of a dark brown liquid which almost resembled coffee, but certainly didn't smell like it.

"Thanks," she said putting the cup on the small table in front of her. DC Worsfold sat down opposite, put his hands together, leant forward and said, "Now, how can I help?"

"As I mentioned on the phone, I'm interested in the report you received about an apparent abduction a couple of weeks ago. It may help the case I'm working on."

"And what case might that be?"

"A suspected murder, more than that I cannot say at this stage," she said.

"The word abduction is a bit strong; I referred to it as a scuffle on the phone."

"You said that a witness mentioned someone being manhandled into a large van," Sarah said.

"There is no evidence for that," said Worsfold defensively.

"What evidence have you looked for, DC Worsfold?" Sarah said stepping up the intensity of her interrogation.

"Call me Ian please. Well, as you are aware, our resources are extremely stretched and, until I identified a possible connection with your case, we were not taking our enquiries any further. We have many more serious crimes to investigate around here, as I am sure you can appreciate."

"Well, Ian," Sarah said, emphasising the word Ian. "The time has come to open up this investigation a little further and I'm here to help and ease your stretched resources."

"What exactly do you want?"

"I need access to all CCTV footage taken from cameras in that area at the time of the reported 'scuffle' please and a quiet room to sit in and review it."

"What, now?" DC Worsfold said in surprise.

"Yes, now - time is of the essence in this case. It may be nearly one thirty in the morning but I'm running out of time. Would that be possible?"

"Yes, I'm sure we can provide that. Follow me, I'll need to speak to Ollie from Tech Support, assuming he's still around."

Ian Worsfold called Ollie as he was about to leave the station and he reluctantly agreed to locate and set the system up for Sarah in the same room where she had spoken to Ian Worsfold a few minutes earlier. Sarah's sweetest smile certainly helped Ian to make his decision.

Within fifteen minutes Ollie had gone home and Sarah sat alone in the small room. It had faded institutional green walls, a high, barred window, metal table and chairs bolted to the floor with a pervading odour of sweat and urine. She sat in front of a TV monitor with a copy of the witness statement in front of her. Around eight thirty on the twenty first of November, it said and she quickly located the relevant disc and inserted it into the player. Almost an hour passed before she found what she was looking for. The reported scuffle was clearly more than that. Through the fuzzy images she could make out the figure of a large, confident man being set upon from behind by three other men. A sack was pulled over the man's head, the rear doors of a white van opened and he was bundled into it. The whole incident took up no more than thirty seconds of recording. She was unable to get any clear identification from the camera angle she was viewing, least of all the registration number of the van which was what she really wanted.

She left the room to look for Ian Worsfold. She found him hammering away on the keyboard of his computer on his desk. He looked up and smiled, "Any luck?"

"Yes. But I need views from other cameras, are there any others in that vicinity do you know?"

"Kingsbury Road, wasn't it? I don't think so, coverage is a bit thin around there. Wait, there may be one on the corner of Watts Avenue, would that be near enough?"

"I don't know, it's your area. Let's take a look," Sarah said. Although she was feeling tired she was also confident that she was onto something.

Having identified the precise time of the incident, it didn't take long to get the different angle from the Watts Avenue camera. Although it didn't show much of the incident itself, it clearly showed the white van pulling up to the kerb and, more importantly, showed the registration number of the van.

"Got it." Sarah shouted to no one in particular in the small room.

She noted the number and immediately took out her mobile hitting the speed dial button for the DVLA.

"I'm off now, thanks for your help," Sarah said, somehow putting on her coat as she spoke on the phone as well as opening the main door.

"No problem, glad we could help," replied DC Worsfold, but Sarah was gone before he had completed his sentence.

*

Andy looked around him for Jane's whereabouts. He was seated in the back seat of a black BMW, alongside one of Eddie's henchmen. Andy thought that he recognised the man as the steel fixer who so expertly dismantled the reinforcement cage to the lift pit on that fateful night ten days ago. But he wasn't sure and he didn't feel that this was the appropriate time to strike up a conversation of any sort.

Andy hadn't initially realised that in fact two BMWs had arrived when he and Jane were pulled over by the police. He had assumed that the doors he heard being shut when he had his face to the rear doors of the van were from the same car. He now realised that Jane was in a second car and he hoped she was heading for the same destination as he was.

His wrists were extremely painful, his arms were pinned behind him, tightly bound together by what he was now certain was a cable tie. The strong sharp plastic was cutting into his flesh every time he made the slightest movement and he quickly established that clasping his hands together was the only way to minimise the discomfort.

The journey in the car wasn't long and Andy's heart sank when he realised he was back at the house where he had sent a man to his possible death through the first floor bannister.

He was roughly pulled out of the car and manhandled down the path and, as he reached the front door, he turned his head sufficiently to see Jane being given the same escort treatment from her car, which had pulled up just behind the one he was travelling in. By the time the steel-faced front door was unlocked Jane was alongside Andy and they were shoved into the hall.

"No special treatment this time. It's the guest quarters for you two," said the man Andy thought was called Taff. Andy also didn't like the ironic emphasis on the word 'guest'.

They were led along the long narrow hall and a door under the stairs was unlocked. They were led down a dark damp flight of concrete steps into what clearly was an old basement. The area at the bottom of the steps was larger than Andy had expected with two solid steel doors on either side of the dark, dank corridor.

The man Andy thought to be Taff took out a bunch of large keys and unlocked one of the doors, he opened it and pushed them both into the small concrete walled room. The cable ties which held their wrists together were roughly cut, freeing their hands and in turn their circulation. The door was quickly slammed shut and locked behind them. Then a small sliding panel in the door was opened from the outside.

"There's a bottle of water there for you; drink some, we don't want you dying of dehydration do we? At least not yet." He laughed to himself and slid the panel shut.

The room was no more than three metres square, it was dimly lit by a light bulb hanging from a frayed wire which would clearly fail any modern day health and safety inspection.

The concrete floor was not covered but the room was furnished with two very shabby armchairs, a small metal framed camp bed and an upturned crate which was supposed to be a table, located between the two chairs. On the crate was a plastic bottle of water and two plastic cups.

Andy looked up at Jane, like him she was rubbing her wrists to ease the pain and help the circulation to restart. But Andy was looking at her face and her clothes. He had time to take in her appearance properly now.

"Jane, please tell me, why are you dressed like that?" he asked as calmly as he could. "Have you joined the New Age movement without telling me? And in case you haven't realised, Glastonbury was months ago."

"That's enough of your sarcasm thank you," Jane replied. "Give me a moment and I'll explain everything."

Andy sat in one of the armchairs and stretched his long legs in front of him.

"What a day," he said. "In context that client meeting wasn't so bad after all."

"Oh, sorry, I forgot all about the client meeting, how did it go?" Jane said conversationally as she sat in the second chair, opened the bottle of water and poured some of it into each of the two cups.

"Jane, we have more pressing things to discuss at the moment than my client meeting. Do you think it's safe to drink this?" Andy said holding the translucent plastic cup up to the light.

"Why? Do you think they'd poison us?"

"Well they've done just about everything else to us, why wouldn't they?"

Jane carefully sniffed it and then said, "I'm parched, I'm drinking this and if I fall to the floor clutching my throat I suggest you leave yours alone."

"Jane, this is no time for gallows humour, I was serious."

By the time he had said that Jane had gulped down the water. Andy waited a few seconds; she was still smiling so he drank his too.

"Well, I think it is time we had a frank discussion don't you?" Andy said, looking down at her tie died jeans he added, "And if you think I'm joining the hippy movement then you can think again."

"Shhhhh," Jane said, putting a finger to her lips, "This room may be bugged," she added quietly.

"Bugged? Bugged?" Andy repeated in an exasperated tone, "What do you mean? Bugged?"

Jane had got out of her chair and was looking up and down each wall and into an air brick fitted at low level.

"I can't see anything, looks okay," she said.

"So now you are an expert on all things to do with spying equipment are you?" Andy said sarcastically.

"Well, yes actually, I did a three week CET course in May last year."

"What? CET. What is that exactly?"

"Counter Espionage Techniques."

"What are you talking about? I think it's time you did some explaining, preferably before I wake from the dream I am having. Or the nightmare more like."

"Calm down, Andy, I'll explain everything but you need to stay calm. What I'm going to say to you will shock and surprise you. Would you please promise me one thing?" Jane said.

"I don't have much choice do I?"

"Just promise me that you will listen to what I have to say without saying a word, no matter how tempting that might be. I'll answer any questions you have when I have finished my explanation. That way it'll be easier for both of us."

"Okay, I promise," said Andy feeling a bit like a six year-old schoolboy. His head was now in a whirl but, despite his confusion, he knew that he had to concentrate on getting them out of the hole they were in.

Jane leant forwards, took a deep breath and started speaking.

"Andy, first of all I shouldn't really tell you any of this at all, but in these circumstances I don't really have a choice. I am not a Forensic Accountant; I am a police officer, an undercover police officer. I have been undercover investigating organised crime for the past eighteen months."

Andy's mouth fell open, he stared at Jane, but honoured his promise and said nothing. Although he was struggling to hold back a gag about how the uniform must have changed.

"It is a horrendously difficult job; it means I have to turn myself into someone completely different. I have to change physically and mentally. When I leave you in the morning I change my hair, add piercings and tattoos and become someone else, as you have clearly noticed. I've been on the inside of an organised crime gang since July last year, primarily to get to the bottom of a number of high profile murders that have been occurring across London. Andy, it is the loneliest place in the world and it's really tough. I cannot talk to, or meet any of my colleagues. I report to just one person; he's a superintendent, he's my controller. There are times when my cover story would become more real than my true story. The lies become truths, and the truths lies. I have to undergo regular psychological testing to check that I am mentally capable of living a lie without losing my mind. Every contact is planned in minute detail and every meeting is highly secretive." She made eye contact with Andy and realised that she had been speaking looking at the plastic cup she held tightly in her hand.

"I was chosen for this because I'm good at my job, very good at my job. We believe there is reason to suspect that senior officers in the force are involved and connected to the murders. From information that I have gathered since I have been on the inside, we now *know* that senior officers are involved, we just don't know who yet."

After she finished speaking Jane took a deep breath, put down her empty cup, placed her hands across her face and sat back in the chair. Relief swept over her, it was as if someone had removed a ton weight from her back. Andy said nothing, scarcely able to take in what he'd heard. But, as he thought things through, bits and pieces fell into place.

"Wow," was all he could say. When he gathered himself together a little more he added, "Well I guess that explains the unusual hours you work and the unexplained trips to Leeds, as well as the driving and self-defence skills."

"Yes, I'm afraid I had to tell a few white lies. At times it's difficult to see where the truth ends and lies begin. I even have to break the law occasionally to give my role credibility."

"So how long have you been a police officer?"

"Since I left school, it's all I've ever wanted to do. From the outset I excelled at everything at Hendon Police College, I even outperformed most of the men. After my first year I was identified as a 'high flyer' and put into a special group. I was one of only three girls in that group at that time."

"So, what happened? If you are undercover why were you tied to the bed?"

"I'm not sure. Something went wrong, maybe they connected me to you or possibly there was a leak from the force somewhere; it does happen. They didn't know for certain I was an undercover officer I don't think, it is just that they didn't trust me."

"Well, as much as I'd like to hear the full story," said Andy, bringing himself back to reality, "We need to get out of here and quickly. Hopefully all your training will help us because I haven't got a clue how we can escape from this stinking hell hole."

"It's not looking good is it?" Jane said as she glanced at the four moss covered concrete walls that surrounded them. "The door and that grill are the only possible exit points unless there is a manhole under the carpet and I don't think that would get us very far."

"What do you think they'll do with us?"

"I don't think they know the answer to that one. If they now know I'm a cop they'll think twice about killing us. Well, me at least. These types of men know what happens to cop killers."

"So, let me get this right. They'll leave you alone but dispose of me? But they now know that you're associated with me. They can't think that's a coincidence."

"They already knew that I knew you, Andy. That's the really unfortunate part. I've had to use you to flush them out."

"Use me? Flush them out? What are you talking about?" Andy spluttered.

"Well, we suspected this gang had been responsible for a number of murders of people thought to be heads of various gangs around London, but we did not have any hard evidence. It is just that these people keep disappearing in mysterious circumstances."

"You mean……..no bodies?" Andy said, thinking back to the early hours of that fateful Friday morning which seemed like it was years ago.

The Concrete Grave

"Yes exactly. Without a body it is very difficult to pin a murder on anybody."

"So, are you saying that you set me up with Eddie?"

"Eddie? What? You know Eddie McNerney?"

Andy's face reddened as he realised what he'd just said. "Well, I wouldn't say know exactly, more that I have been unwittingly dragged into his murky little world."

"That is what was supposed to have happened, I didn't realise it had actually worked until you told me about that cash bonus you got."

"Supposed to have happened?" repeated Andy in a confused tone.

Jane sighed, took a deep breath and was just about to elaborate when they heard the door to their cell being unlocked.

"Tea up," said a cheerful voice as the large steel door slowly creaked open. "I don't want anyone accusing us of lacking in hospitality." The solid man was carrying a tray with two mugs on it and he had pushed the door open with his right foot. Just as the door was about halfway open a loud commotion broke out in the house somewhere above them. The noise was apparently coming from the ground floor and it sounded as though someone was battering the front door down accompanied by a lot of hysterical shouting. The man with a tray of tea turned his head away from his two captors and shouted up the stairs, "What's going on up there Jim?"

The man had made a big mistake; Jane was trained not to miss an opportunity when presented with one. She leapt from the chair and caught him totally off guard. She kicked up at the underside of the tray the man was holding, sending the two mugs of scalding hot tea into his face and eyes. The man screamed and bent double bringing his hands up to his eyes as Jane neatly followed up with a sharp karate chop to the man's exposed neck. He fell onto the concrete floor face down with barely a murmur.

"Nice work," Andy said, still sitting in the armchair admiring her action.

"Come on, this way - we haven't a moment to lose," Jane said.

They ran through the open door of the cell they were in but, instead of turning left and returning the way they had come in, Jane dragged Andy to the right along the short corridor to what appeared to be a dead end.

"Where are you going?" Andy said, "This leads to a dead end."

"My aunt lived in a house like this and if I remember correctly there was a coal cellar at the end…..there it is." Jane shouted in triumph.

"We're not going to get far from there," protested Andy.

Jane ignored him and, kicking open the rotting half height door in the wall, she quickly bent over and scrambled through the low narrow opening. Andy followed, it was much harder for him due to his bulk but he just made it. The commotion above them was continuing but appeared to be dying down and Jane knew that they didn't have much time.

"What now?" Andy said.

"To get the coal into these cellars it always came down a chute - we just need to find where it is and climb up it."

"And how large are these chutes, am I likely to fit in it?"

"That is exactly what we're about to find out, Andy." With that Jane, who had been feeling her way along the wall, suddenly disappeared from view. The light was very poor but Andy was able to make out an opening about sixty centimetres square at floor level, Jane had clearly found the chute and was making her way up it. Andy heard the sound of footsteps running along the corridor followed by a loud voice.

"Ted are you okay? What's going on?"

Andy didn't hesitate, he forced his way through the opening and started scrambling up the concrete chute which was at an angle of about forty five degrees. He stopped suddenly as his head make contact with Jane who had stopped above him.

"Andy, I can't shift the cover. It's wedged, or has something on it."

"Here let me try," said Andy. He squeezed past Jane as far as he could and stretched out his long arm. He knew they didn't have much time left and so with all his might he gave one almighty push against the underside of the cast iron manhole cover. It lifted up, and with Jane's help they were able to topple it over, the cold night air rushed into their faces. They quickly climbed through the narrow opening and looked around to get their bearings.

"We've done it," said Andy and they turned down the passage between two houses and ran towards the street. They started to pick up speed and then, just as they got to the front garden, Jane stumbled and fell flat on her face. Andy was too close behind to take avoiding action and fell down on top of her. He quickly looked up as a powerful torch was switched on and shone into their faces.

"Armed police. You two are going nowhere," said a calm but firm female voice which belonged to someone who was leaning against the wall of the next door house and pointing a gun at both of them.

It was clear that all their assailant had done was to thrust out a timely foot and trip Jane up, but neither of them was in any position to challenge this confident lady.

"On your feet, slowly, this gun is loaded and I'm quite prepared to use it," she said.

"Do what she says, Andy, this is no time for heroics," said Jane. The lady moved forward and shone the torch in Andy's face and then into Jane's.

"Jane? What the hell? Is it you? Been to a fancy dress party have we?" she said.

"Sarah? What you doing here? And don't you start on the sarcasm, I've had enough of that for one evening."

"I might ask you the same question," Sarah replied.

"Look, I hate to interrupt this old girls reunion but as none of us now know the good guys from the bad guys, I think we should get out of here," Andy interrupted.

"Quick, this way, my car is in a side street," Sarah said, turning on her heels and cutting across the corner of the front garden of the next door house. Andy stopped and saw two police cars parked in the road with their blue lights still flashing. Now he understood what had caused the commotion, and after their latest interaction with the police, he had no idea whose side they were on. Regardless, he had no time to think any more as Jane and Sarah were already thirty metres ahead of him. He took a deep breath and chased after them.

Chapter Ten

Andy reached the parked car and started to open the back door just as Sarah Thompson floored the throttle. The light blue Ford Focus shot away from the kerb and Andy had to hang on extremely tightly to the inside door handle, as he was propelled on to the back seat, with the door slamming shut as the car sped away.

"We need to find somewhere to talk," said Sarah.

"Where is the nearest station to here?" Jane asked.

"No, I don't think it's a good idea to go to a police station. Walls have ears and all that."

"Where are we going to find somewhere at three o'clock in the morning where we can have a quiet chat?" Jane said.

"There are some large hotels at Canary Wharf that'll still be open, we will head there. The Marriott is probably the best and it's not too far."

After her speedy getaway Sarah had moderated her speed and was driving much more sedately now in order not to attract any unwanted attention. Andy had just about managed to get himself comfortable on the back seat and fasten his seatbelt when he said, "Okay, okay what's going on here? How on earth do you two know each other?"

"Hendon, we trained together," it was Sarah who answered. "We found ourselves in the top group together, Jane was top in everything, as I expect you already know."

"I didn't even know Jane was a policewoman until a couple of hours ago, but that's another story. What I'd like to know is why you arranged a Hendon reunion in this part of London at three o'clock in the morning?"

"We didn't arrange anything, Andy." It was Jane who answered. "Anyway I wasn't top in everything. You were always the best shot," she continued, turning to Sarah to deliver her second sentence.

Andy decided not to pursue his questioning at this point. Hopefully things would become clearer when they reached the hotel. He looked out of the window, amazed at how quickly and dramatically the London landscape had changed from rundown Victorian slums one minute to prestige, glass-clad office blocks and luxury waterside apartments the next.

Sarah knew exactly where she was going and turned left down a ramp into an underground car park. She took a ticket, the barrier lifted and they easily found a parking space in the half empty car park.

They got out of the car and made their way up some stairs which led directly into a very large reception area. The long check-in counter, which would normally be staffed by several receptionists, was empty, as was the whole area.

"May I help you?" a voice said from behind.

They all turned in unison to see a smartly uniformed concierge, walking towards them.

"Yes, we'd like somewhere quiet to sit please. Oh, and three coffees too if possible," said Sarah.

"Certainly madam," said the concierge as he gave a suspicious glance at Jane hoping her attire wasn't going to lead to any inappropriate behaviour, not to mention that she and Andy were covered in dirt and grime following their escapade in the coal cellar. Pointing with his right arm extended, he led the way to the far end of the reception area. They walked across the marble floor on to a red carpeted area, down some steps to a very discreet and empty lounge. They sat in a corner area on some very comfortable looking chairs.

Andy sat down and stretched his long legs out in front of him as he was overcome by a wave of tiredness. He glanced at his watch, it was twenty past three in the morning.

"I need to be on site in four hours," he said.

Jane laughed as if it was the funniest joke she'd heard in years.

"I'm serious," Andy said, "I have a busy day tomorrow, or today rather, and I need to be there."

"No way are you going to work; you won't be safe there in any case," Jane said.

"Not safe? What are you talking about?"

"We need to assess where we are with this operation and until I have clarity on who is where, you won't be going anywhere, even home." Jane said this in an authoritative voice and then turned to Sarah, "So, what brought you to our little abode at such an unearthly hour? Explain please."

"I'm working on a case, well, until four hours ago I was anyway."

"How long have you been on this case?" Jane asked.

"Not long, a couple of weeks, got absolutely nowhere until last night, then moments later, bingo, we were pulled off the case."

"You still haven't answered my question, how did you find us?"

"I tracked down a suspect vehicle linked to our investigation which was registered to that address, called for backup just in case, and well, you saw the reception we got."

"It wasn't a white transit van by any chance was it?" said Andy, who had been listening intently to what was being said.

"Well yes, it was as a matter of fact. How did you know?"

"Lucky guess?" Andy said, wishing he'd kept his mouth shut.

"What's your story, Jane?" Sarah said, ignoring Andy altogether.

"Sarah," Jane said, "You need to know that I am undercover in an operation tracing a suspect gang. Andy is my partner who has been working with us to assist me."

"Working with you? Since when? Sarah, I'm just a humble project manager, doing my best to build a new school for a very demanding client in a very dodgy area of East London." Andy stopped as a young girl arrived with a tray carrying a large cafetiere of coffee and three cups. She placed the tray on the table in front of them.

"Would you like me to set up a tab?" she said in an east European accent.

"No, we'll pay by cash," said Sarah handing her a twenty pound note.

"I don't expect you'll get much change from that here," Andy said somewhat unnecessarily.

The Concrete Grave

The young waitress left and Sarah took up the conversation. "So let me get this right, Jane, you've been undercover with a suspect gang; that at least explains your unusual dress sense and painful looking piercings, especially that one" she said pointing to a diamond like stone that went through her top lip just under her nose.

"It's all fake – clever I grant you, but fake nonetheless," Jane said defensively, carefully removing the item.

"And what is Andy's role? Has he been helping? Are you undercover too, Andy?"

"No," said Andy loudly, "I told you I'm just a builder." He then reached out, pressed the cafetiere and poured out three cups of rich smelling coffee.

"Well," said Sarah slowly, "The unit I'm working in has been set up to concentrate on gangland crime which is increasing faster than at any time since the nineteen sixties. The most recent disappearance is a certain Tommy Sutcliffe." Sarah was immediately distracted by a loud choking sound emitted by Andy as he leant forward discharging a mouthful of coffee across the table in front of him. "Are you alright, Andy?" Jane asked.

"Yes, fine, it's hotter than I expected that's all," replied Andy conscious of the blood in his cheeks, he did not want to look either of them in the eyes.

"What division are you in, Jane?" continued Sarah as Andy used some paper serviettes to mop up his spilt coffee.

"I shouldn't be telling you any of this, but I get the feeling that by joining forces we may get somewhere," Jane said.

"Anyway we go back a long time together," Sarah said.

"I'm part of the IIU."

"The what? I've never heard of it."

"Not many people have, it's the Internal Investigations Unit, a top secret team set up in the wake of all the recent scandals relating to police corruption. There is a strong feeling that these gangland disappearances or murders are linked to senior officers in the Met. I can't go into details, we have strong suspicions but we don't yet have any firm evidence. My brief was to get close to the gang and see if I could discover any links to the force. As yet I haven't been successful, but I feel we're close."

"So what were you doing in the house?" Sarah said.

Suddenly there was a loud commotion in the reception area of the hotel. All three turned to see what was going on. Four men in dinner jackets and bow ties had entered the hotel and were singing at the tops of their voices. One of the men held an opened bottle of Veuve Clicquot champagne.

"Now you're gonna believe us, we've gone and won the cup!" The chant was slurred and tuneless and Andy noticed that one of the men held a crystal trophy in his hand.

The group was staggering across the marble floor. One of the men had his arm around the shoulders of another, but it was unclear who was supporting who. As they made their way to the lift one of the men noticed Andy, Sarah and

Jane and, smiling inanely, he made his way uncertainly towards them.

"Hello ladies," he said loudly, completely ignoring Andy. "Want some company do you?" As he reached them his left leg caught the side of the two-seater settee that Jane and Sarah were sitting on and he nearly toppled into Sarah's lap. He just stopped himself and ended up sitting on the arm of the settee with his left arm across the back behind Sarah.

"We won the trophy tonight, we did," the man slurred, breathing a foul stale smell of alcohol over the three of them. He was middle aged, his bow tie was untied and hanging down unevenly across the front of his wine stained dress shirt.

"What trophy might that be?" Andy asked. Jane looked sternly at Andy, annoyed that he'd entered into conversation with the man.

"The Environmental Health and Safety Award for projects up to five million pounds," the man proudly announced. Just then he was joined by his colleagues who all seemed in a similar state of inebriation.

"Come on, Malc, leave the good people alone," one of the less inebriated men said.

"No, I think they're looking for some company, aren't you ladies?" Malc said.

"Actually, we were having a private conversation and we wish to be left alone thank you," Sarah said almost too politely.

"Wish to be left alone, do you?" Repeated Malc, suddenly becoming much more aggressive. "You don't know what you're missing. Come on, join me in a glass of bubbly." Malc leant across and attempted to pour champagne into Sarah's half empty coffee cup, he missed and champagne ended up on the floor between the coffee table and the settee.

"Oopps," was all Malc could say before he started giggling.

"Come on, Malc, off to bed with you," said the other man who was clearly starting to worry that things may be getting out of hand.

"Come on darling, just a little cuddle," Malc said as he tried to put his arms around Sarah. Sarah had had enough and, as quick as a flash, she grabbed the man's right wrist, stood up and twisted his arm behind his back with one hand. With the other hand she removed her warrant card and she thrust it in front of his face.

"You've got five seconds to remove yourself from here or you're under arrest. Understand?" Sarah said calmly.

"Okay, okay, I was just trying to be friendly," Malc said in a tone that suggested Sarah's approach had sobered him up quicker than anything Andy had ever seen before.

"I didn't realise you were old bill, did I?"

"Obviously not," said Sarah.

Two of his colleagues, realising that things had got a little too heavy for comfort, grabbed an arm each and Malc was dragged unceremoniously across the floor. The remaining colleague said, "I'm so sorry about that, can I get you another drink or anything?"

"No, we're fine, a little privacy is all we would ask," said Sarah.

"Fine, fine," said the man backing away, "Goodnight then." He turned and quickly joined his colleagues, who have managed to drag Malc into a lift. The lift doors closed behind them and silence returned.

"Men." Sarah said, "You'd think men of that age would know better."

"A boy's night out," Andy said, "Probably only get the chance once a year. You should've seen the expression on his face when you held your ID in front of him. Wish I'd got a photo."

"Unfortunately, they'll be talking about it for years to come I suspect. Anyway where were we? Yes, what were you two doing in that house?"

After a short silence, as she gathered her thoughts following the interruption Jane said, "We'd been looking for some time at ways to get me closer to a gang that we had identified as doing the hits and disposing of the bodies. I managed to infiltrate the gang and heard them talking about using construction sites as the means of disposal, so I immediately thought of Andy. We needed someone we knew would testify against them and Andy, being the upright and moral person that he is, fitted the bill nicely. I told Eddie, the leader of the gang, that I had met Andy in a local pub and that he had told me about his money problems. They were delighted and of course it enhanced my position with them."

"What? So you set me up? All this about the credit card was fabricated?"

"It was not exactly fabricated. More part of the plan. I needed to create a desire in you to encourage you to accept an offer that otherwise you probably wouldn't have. By the way, I really did use those gambling sites and lost that money. Actually it was harder to lose than you think. I kept winning at the start."

"So, I assume that the Met will play off my credit card bill?" Andy said, suddenly getting very angry.

"Of course," continued Jane in a matter of fact way, "I'll put it on my expenses; it won't be a problem."

"So let me understand this," interrupted Sarah trying to get them back on track, "You set Andy up so that when he was offered the chance of some quick money he'd take it. I get that. But how did you infiltrate the gang and gain their trust?"

"It took a while. I hung around in their local pubs, pretending to want drugs. They needed a skivvy for their house and selected me for the role. It took a few weeks, not a lot of fun I can assure you."

"And has your cover been blown now?"

"Yes, I think so. They may not be certain that I am a police officer but they don't trust me now, that's for sure."

"Why what happened?"

"Well, the gang were worried that Andy was having second thoughts about what he'd done and wanted to come clean. They were worried that he'd go to the police, so to stop him they decided to kidnap his girlfriend. I found out about their plan and realised that it would also blow my cover, so I kept clear of our house in Hampshire so that they couldn't track me down. I had to spend more time with them in their hovel at Shackleton Road as a result."

"So that's where you were last weekend and your plan to involve me worked like clockwork. Thanks a bunch," said Andy tired and exasperated.

"I'm sorry, Andy, I quickly regretted what I had done, but by then it was too late - you were already on the hook. Although I didn't know it at the time."

"So did you know that I'd been given some money then?"

"Well, I worked it out as soon as you told me about your bonus which had been paid in cash; no company does that any more. Anyway I was then caught eavesdropping while they were talking about it, so I had to be much more careful. I wasn't certain, but I suspected that the plan was working. They then somehow worked out that I was closer to you than I had let on and that I was your partner which, not surprisingly, caused them to become highly suspicious. Fortunately they never saw me dressed as anything other than I am now. But it caused them to realise that I hadn't been telling them the whole truth, so they kept me under lock and key after that. They then told you that I was a captive to discourage you from going to the police. This worked quite well until you recognised their van on your way home from work last night."

"Oh dear. So, my heroic rescue screwed things up for you then did it?" Andy asked apologetically.

"No, not really, quite the reverse actually." Jane hastily reassured him. "The surprising part was when you came from nowhere to rescue me. I wasn't expecting that but it may have helped move things on." A moment's silence as this started to sink in. "Who is your DI, Sarah?"

"The honourable Jeremy Lloyd-Brown," said Sarah, "Jez to his friends."

"What name did you say?" Andy suddenly interjected.

"Jez. Everyone from the cleaner to the Chief Constable calls him that."

"Why do you ask, Andy?" Jane said, sensing something odd.

"Well, as you two have been comparing notes, I was thinking that it was about time that I came clean. The name you just mentioned has confirmed it."

"What you mean? Do you know Jez?" Sarah asked.

"Not exactly," said Andy, "But I think he fits in somewhere. Let me explain; My involvement started about two weeks ago, following the discovery of the credit card bill. Well, the very next day I got a call on my mobile from a man called Eddie. I did know him as he had supplied some labour for me on site. Good quality labour too I might add. Well, Eddie seemed to know that I had money problems and asked me to meet him in the pub near to site. He said that he had got the answer to all my prayers."

"Frankly, I was a bit surprised that you agreed to meet up with Eddie." Jane interrupted.

"Yes, looking back I'm not sure why I did."

"Why didn't you tell me?"

"Why should I? I was worried, embarrassed, ashamed even."

"Carry on, Andy. I think I know where this might be going." Sarah said.

"Well, I met Eddie at the Prince of Wales pub. He bought me a drink and asked me to do a little job for him."

"What sort of job?"

"Well, he wanted me to dispose of a 'package,' I think he called it. Well, of course I imagined a small box the size of a shoebox or maybe smaller. It turned out to be a little bigger than that."

"Why on earth did you agree?" Sarah said.

"I didn't really, at least not initially. While I was thinking it over Eddie thrust a brown envelope at me, saying 'same again when you've delivered.' He got up and walked away leaving me sitting there holding on to what turned out to be five thousand pounds in crisp, new fifty pound notes. I didn't really have a choice. We needed the money and in one stroke it would have cleared our debt. We were both worried sick about the situation and I thought, what harm could it do? Helping a poor man to dispose of his 'package' isn't a crime." Andy emphasised the word 'package' and stopped speaking as the waitress returned to the table.

"Any more coffees?" she asked cheerily.

"Yes please, same again, do you have any food? I'm starving." Andy added.

"Shortbread biscuits is all we have at this time of night I'm afraid," the waitress replied.

"They'll be fine, thanks," Andy said.

"Okay, now I'm getting impatient. What was the package Andy?" Sarah asked.

The Concrete Grave

"Tommy Sutcliffe."

The area they were sitting in was large, it was close to four o'clock in the morning, but you could have heard a pin drop. Jane looked at Andy, her mouth half open and then to Sarah, who was looking puzzled.

It was Jane who broke the silence, "Are you saying that you disposed of the body, Andy? I honestly wasn't sure. I was getting concerned that things were getting out of control. I thought I would be more aware of the gang's activities than I actually was."

"Well that was your plan wasn't it? It wasn't me anyway, well not exactly. All I had to do was open the site in the middle of the night to allow Eddie and his henchmen to dispose of this package. I didn't know it was a body until they carried it to the lift pit."

"How did you know it was Tommy Sutcliffe?"

"Well, I didn't at the time, but when they were carrying the package, which was wrapped in black tarpaulin, one of the men slipped and an arm dropped down. I noticed that a thumb was missing from one of his hands. A few days later in *The Metro* I read about this missing gangland head and they called him 'One Thumb Tommy,' so I put two and two together."

"And kept quiet," Jane said.

"Of course I kept quiet." Andy said, his voice rising in volume. "What did you expect me to do? Hold a press conference in front of Buckingham Palace?"

Sarah laughed at the thought, "Now, that would have been something."

"Look at things from my perspective. I suddenly found myself part of a group of men that had placed a body in the bottom of a lift shaft and I had ordered the concrete which covered him up forever. I then received ten thousand pounds cash for doing it. I had no idea how I got myself into that position, but I certainly had even less idea how I was going to get myself out of it. But you knew all along what was going on?" he said turning to face Jane.

"Yes, well not entirely, but I sensed that the plan was beginning to work."

"Jane, I was going through hell. I was frightened at what might happen, not just to me, but to you as well. Don't forget, at that time, you were an accountant as far as I knew. I didn't know who to talk to."

"Why didn't you talk to me?"

"I nearly did on a number of occasions, but I just thought you'd make me turn myself in and return the money. I'd be put inside, and we would still have a huge debt. Now it looks like I'll be put inside but we won't have a huge debt."

Jane was shaking her head, smiling, "You won't get put in prison, Andy, it was all set up. You have played a key role in helping us get to the bottom of this, and we are not far away now. Providing you will testify against them, you'll come out of this a hero."

"Are you certain? I really want to do something to redeem myself. I can't believe I got sucked into this. Your plan certainly worked, and I am very glad you are not a compulsive gambler. It'll take me a while to get used to living with a police officer though; but one question."

"Sure, what is it?"

"Why did you have to come up with an elaborate plan to draw me in, why not just tell me the truth and ask me to help?"

"Andy, it was vital that at that stage I maintained my undercover status, which meant that only my controller knew what I was doing. Also, do you really think you would've acted naturally with Eddie if you had known what was really going on?"

"No, I suppose I wouldn't have, I never was a great actor."

"Eddie would've smelt a rat immediately I am sure," Jane said.

"Yes, I guess so." Andy admitted, "One other thing does puzzle me however, I really should be feeling angry with you at being set-up; but the strange thing is I'm not. It's as if this episode has shown me the strength of my feelings towards you. I must say though, I'm really glad this is all out in the open now. It's like a huge load has been lifted off my shoulders. I hope this won't change the way we feel about each other."

"Yes, I feel the same having told you all this too. It's been a huge pressure on me as well and coming clean to you has come as a great relief. And no, I hope it won't change our feelings towards each other. I'm so sorry for putting you through all of this, but I'm still the same Jane you met that day on Waterloo station, and I'll be even more her now I won't have to be undercover."

"Well I'm glad to hear that. I should have told you what was going on ages ago," Andy said as he moved closer to her giving her a huge hug, burying his face into her tattooed shoulder. As he pulled away he said, "I hope that tattoo comes off easily. It doesn't suit you."

"Coffee," said the waitress as she lowered the tray on to the table, "And some shortbread," she passed Andy a large unopened packet of shortbread. "You looked hungry," she said.

"You've got an admirer there," Sarah said as the waitress went away.

"Now, Andy, you said you knew Jez, or at least woke up when I mentioned his name. Where do you know him from?"

"I don't know him, I recognised the name, that's all, it may be nothing. Eddie has been threatening me since the body was put in the lift pit. Clearly he was worried that I'd spill the beans. A few days ago, early in the morning, he accosted me as I was approaching site. He held my arm tight, looked me in the eye, sort of threatened me and told me not to do anything stupid. Anyway, just as we were concluding discussions, or rather after I'd finished listening to his ranting, his mobile phone rang and as he walked away, he answered it and I heard, well I'm pretty sure I heard him say the name 'Jez'. Kind of unusual, so I remembered it. 'Yes Jez', Eddie said; then he walked away."

"Well, that's mega," Jane said, "Jeremy Lloyd-Brown involved with Eddie McNerney. Incredible."

"Hang on a minute," interrupted Sarah, "Don't jump to conclusions, he's not the only person in London called Jez. Although, I have to confess that he has been behaving rather strangely lately and was particularly off with me when I wanted to pursue the Tommy Sutcliffe case after he had told me it was closed. Can you remember anything else at all that Eddie might have said whilst talking on the phone, Andy?"

"No, he was walking away from me as he spoke and I didn't take much notice after that in any case," Andy said.

"Could he be our inside man I wonder?" Jane said.

"Well, there's only one way to find out. Come on drink up, we've got work to do," said Sarah.

"What at this time? I'm shattered," Andy said looking at his watch.

"True, we can't do much for a few hours, let's see if we can get a couple of rooms here," Sarah said.

"And just how are we going to afford that?"

"Expenses, Andy. Under these circumstances there won't be a problem," Sarah replied confidently.

The hotel wasn't fully booked and the man who checked them in didn't think anything strange in two women and a man booking two rooms at four fifteen in the morning. Jane paid an extortionate price for three travel packs of toiletries which included, among other things, tooth brush and toothpaste, which, to her, were the top priority.

While Andy was waiting for Jane and Sarah to sort out the rooms he discreetly sent a text to Dave letting him know that he'd be late in that morning. Regardless of what

Jane had said, he had a job to do and he wasn't the sort of person to let anyone down.

They found their rooms, next to each other on the eleventh floor. As Andy entered the room he removed his shoes and laid on the bed. He was asleep in seconds.

Chapter Eleven

Jez walked along the unlit road, his hands thrust deep into his pockets to protect them from the cold night air. It was the last place he wanted to be in the early hours of the morning. The towering, dark railway arches always looked more threatening in the dark.

It was surprisingly quiet. He looked up and saw the soft orange glow of a cigarette about fifty metres ahead. He slowly approached the smoker, who thought he was concealed in the shadows of the railway arch.

"Hello, Eddie," Jez said. "Cocked up again did you?"

"It wasn't anything to do with me, Jez, honest." It was the best response that Eddie could think of.

"So who was it to do with then? David Cameron?"

"Who? No, of course not," Eddie said unnecessarily.

"Look, Eddie," said Jez feeling anger rising up inside him. "That was the very last time I'm going to bail you out. This business is getting a little too hot for my liking and your unending incompetence isn't helping my blood pressure."

"Sorry, Jez," said Eddie, deciding to take a different tack. "I think we have a grass in the team."

"Any idea who?"

"Not for certain, but I'll find out for sure. Could be Taff, never did trust him. He has a gambling habit and is always short of cash." Eddie had no intention of telling Jez that he'd allowed a girl to infiltrate their gang, he was angry enough with him as it was.

The Concrete Grave

"Well you'd better make sure it doesn't happen again or you could be in for a long stretch." Jez stopped speaking and watched a lone cyclist slowly go past. "What on earth do you think anyone would be doing cycling around here at this time of night?" Jez mused, not expecting an answer. "I've got one last job for you, Eddie, then that's it."

"Are you sure it's safe to do another, Jez?"

"No, not at all, but you don't have an option now do you?" Jez said, pushing a large brown envelope into Eddie's chest. "Everything you need to know is in there."

"When?"

"As soon as. Get this one out of the way and we can all lie low for a while."

"How much?"

"The usual, fifty grand. Half of it is in there. The other half is yours upon successful delivery. Why did you ask? Were you expecting a pay rise?" Jez said sarcastically.

"Well, with the heat on as it is I don't think it is unreasonable to ask for a bit more - let's call it danger money," said Eddie.

"Well, I do think it's unreasonable," Jez said, gritting his teeth and grabbing Eddie by the throat, the sudden force of his action sending Eddie hard up against the decaying brickwork behind him. "Very unreasonable. After what you did last night I've half a mind to pay you less, not more. It took me three calls to get you released. I'm putting my head over the parapet a little too often for my liking," said Jez his voice rising in volume as his anger grew.

"One other thing," Eddie said reluctantly.

"What?"

"What do you want doing with this fella Andy and his lady friend?"

"Nothing. They'll not bother us any more after what they've been through, I'm sure of that. Anyway you'll have enough on your plate sorting that one out," Jez said pointing at the envelope that Eddie was still clutching into his chest.

"Okay. I'll call you when it's done."

Jez didn't hear Eddie's parting comment as he had already stepped out of the arch and was striding back up the street in the direction he had come from.

*

Andy awoke with a start, and sat up in bed not knowing where he was. He looked around the smart new hotel room which looked the complete opposite of Mrs Massoud's establishment where he had stayed just ten days before. He gradually remembered the events of the previous night.

"Ah, you're awake are you?" Jane said. She was standing at the end of the bed with a towel around her having just had a shower.

"What time is it?"

"Nearly half past nine."

"Doesn't feel like it to me. Still feels like the middle of the night. What happens now?"

"Well, I suggest you have a shower. Sarah's coming here in ten minutes and we'll plan the next step."

The Concrete Grave

"What about breakfast? I'm starving."

"You're always thinking about your stomach, Andy," said Jane with a smile. "You can have breakfast, it is all included in the price so you may just as well."

Andy had his shower and got his trousers on just in time as Sarah knocked on the door. Jane quickly let her in.

"Morning," she said cheerily. "Sleep well?"

"Considering the circumstances, yes I did thanks," said Andy.

Sarah went across to the window. "Nice view," she said looking down on the canal below and the ornate footbridge which took commuters to their work and tourists to the cafes and shops on the other side. She turned and sat in the chair next to the flat screen television. Jane, who had dressed and was drying her hair, sat on the end of the bed.

"So," said Jane, "If it is Jeremy Lloyd-Brown, how are we going to prove it?"

"The first thing I want to do is to check his mobile phone records and see if we can get a match with Eddie's number. Andy, you said that you thought you heard Eddie ring Jez, didn't you?"

"Yes, I'm sure that's the name he said."

"We just need Eddie's number, then we'll run a check on it to see if he has called or received a call from Jez. How do we get that?"

"Not a problem, I've got it," Andy said taking out his Nokia E71. "He rang and texted me loads of times." Andy's fingers quickly accessed the received calls section of his phone and gave the eleven digit number to Sarah.

"Great, thanks, I need to get back to the office and run this through the computer. What will you do, Jane?"

"I'm not sure. I need to contact my controller first. I don't know whether my cover has been blown or not. Either way I don't want to take any chances, and I certainly don't fancy going back to the house."

"Well, if you girls will excuse me," said Andy, "I'm going to get some breakfast before it's too late. Won't be long." Andy gathered his things and left the room.

"Jane, why don't you make use of the facilities here, there's a good spa in the basement. You've had a pretty tough few days. I'll give you a call as soon as I come up with something."

"Okay, I might just do that. Not much more I can do at this stage."

*

Andy walked out of the lift and across the foyer, which seemed to have sprung into life since he was there the night before. Despite his hunger and the enticing smells coming from the restaurant, he headed straight towards the revolving doors. Once outside he made his way to Canary Wharf tube station. Canning Town station was just two stops along the Jubilee Line, within thirty minutes he was back on site.

"Decided to have a lay in did you?" said Dave as Andy entered the office, "A duvet day they call it now, I think."

The Concrete Grave

"Dave, a duvet day is when you stay in bed for the whole day, not when you arrive a little late, as I have just done," Andy said.

"Don't worry, you've not missed much."

"How many bricklayers have we got in today?"

"Sixteen, one more than yesterday, they're making good progress. If the rain holds off we'll be up to roof level by Friday as we'd planned. How did your dinner with Steve go?"

Dinner with Steve? Andy thought. Was that really just last night? So much had happened since then that it felt like weeks ago.

"Oh, fine thanks. We had a nice steak too, we put the world to rights and topped if off with an excellent bottle of red wine."

"Is that all? Did he help you? You certainly seem more cheerful today anyway."

"Yes, I guess I am, I can certainly see things with greater clarity now."

"Good, then you can sort out that useless procurement department of ours and get them to place the order for the roof covering pronto, because if they're not ready to start next week we've wasted our time chasing the bricklayers uphill and down dale."

"Okay, I'll give Ray a call."

Andy dialled a number on his mobile phone, he felt surprisingly uplifted to be back at work after everything that had happened the night before.

*

Sarah arrived in the office just after ten o'clock, yet there was only one other person there. Toby was at his desk typing away at his keyboard. He looked up, raised his right hand to acknowledge her presence but kept on typing, totally absorbed in what he was doing.

Sarah picked up the phone on her desk and quickly punched in five numbers.

"I need some mobile phone records and quickly please," she gave the person on the other end of the phone Eddie's mobile number with her email address.

"How long will it take? Really? Is that all? Great thanks."

"How long were you told?" Toby asked, suddenly taking an interest.

"No more than ten minutes. Why?"

"Well, I made the same request last week and I was told no more than ten minutes and then waited all day. So don't get your hopes up."

"We'll see. Maybe my feminine charms will do the trick," Sarah said, bending down to turn on her computer. "Would you like some coffee?"

"If you are making some, yes please."

"Where is everyone?"

"At some briefing on a new job, Islington or somewhere I think?"

Sarah swore loudly. "I knew there was something I should be doing," she said, remembering Jez's orders of the previous night. Sarah thought for a moment, "I thought it was supposed to be here anyway?"

"Moved to Islington according to the email that I had a copy of," Toby said.

Sarah's computer was now up and running. She opened her emails and sure enough, the briefing had been moved. So at least she had half an excuse if pressed.

She went to the small kitchen area and made two cups of instant coffee. She gave one to Toby who acknowledged it by just giving a cursory thumbs up.

Sarah returned to her computer. "Bingo. Less than seven minutes, not bad. feminine charm wins again." Toby grunted and chose not to comment.

She opened the attachment to the email containing the information she had requested. She checked Jez's mobile number on her phone then she scrolled down the list of numbers that Eddie had dialled in the last two weeks. He had certainly made a lot of calls, but none to the number that she had for Jez. Did he have a second phone? She'd never seen him with one but she was annoyed with herself for even thinking that Jez would be stupid enough to use his police issue mobile phone for calling known criminals. Somehow she had to get the number of his private mobile.

"What are you studying so intently?" a sudden voice said from behind her.

Sarah had been concentrating so hard on the spread sheet on her screen that she hadn't heard Jez enter the office, let alone walk up behind her.

"And, where were you this morning? I told you, eight o'clock at Islington."

"You told me eight o'clock *here*," Sarah challenged.

"Didn't you get the email changing the venue?"

"Yes, but didn't see it until a few minutes ago. Sorry, Jez," she said.

"No worries, I'll update you in a minute. What was that you were looking at?"

"Oh, just some mobile phone records, relating to an old case."

"Not Tommy Sutcliffe I hope. I told you to drop that one."

"No, not at all," she half laughed to cover up the lie. "Jez, I tried to ring you last night, your phone was off."

"Oh, yes when I'm at home I sometimes turn it off otherwise I never get a moment's peace, you know how it is."

"Do you have a personal mobile, in case anything urgent comes up?" Sarah was bluffing now but her charms were having an effect on Jez.

"Sure, but I don't give the number out. That would rather defeat the object of having a second phone, wouldn't it?"

"What, not even to me? You know I wouldn't abuse it, for emergencies only."

"Okay. I can't remember the number, I hardly ever use it." Jez took a second mobile phone from an inside jacket pocket. He studied the screen on his top of the range iPhone. "Here it is," and he gave out the number to her which she hurriedly wrote on a nearby Post-It note. He turned and went into his office closing the door behind him.

Sarah could hardly breathe as she checked the number Jez had just given to her against those listed on Eddie's record of calls. It wasn't long before she hit the jackpot. There on the list of eleven digit numbers was Jez's number several times all called during the past two weeks. It was all she could do to keep quiet but she had no intention of drawing attention to herself. She picked up her mug of coffee and pondered her next move.

She could hardly believe that Jez would be mixed up with someone like Eddie McNerney, but the evidence was there to be seen.

It wasn't long before Sarah had decided what to do; she always had been impulsive and that wasn't about to change now. She printed out a couple of sheets of Eddie McNerney's mobile phone call record, gathered some other papers together and went over to the closed door of Jez's office. She gently knocked on the door.

"Come in," said a voice from inside the room.

Sarah put her head around the door, smiling her sweetest smile, "Is now a good time to catch up on the Islington briefing?" she asked.

Jez looked up, returning the smile, he said, "Sure, come in."

The Concrete Grave

Sarah put a hand into her jacket pocket and felt the reassuring presence of her mobile phone.

"It won't take long, as usual there is not much to go on at this stage."

Jez gave Sarah a summary of the briefing, explaining that there had been a rapid rise in drug related crime in a small area to the north of Islington. Two known criminals were believed to be connected to it, and their brief was to find out exactly what was going on.

"Well, that should be enough to keep you going," said Jez deliberately closing the meeting. "Any questions?"

"Just one," Sarah replied, "Why have you received seven phone calls from a certain Eddie McNerney in the past two weeks?"

"What are you talking about, Sarah? I don't understand, what is this?"

"Jez, I have evidence linking Eddie McNerney with the disappearance of Tommy Sutcliffe, and evidence linking you with Eddie McNerney." She held up the two sheets of paper with the telephone records on.

"This is nonsense," said Jez, clearly disturbed by the direction this conversation was taking. "Did you get my personal mobile number so you could run a check? Why you bitch!"

"Steady, Jez, you don't want a sexual harassment case against you as well do you?" Sarah said calmly.

"If you must know, Sarah, that scum bag McNerney is one of my informants. He gives me tip offs if anything big is going down. What of it?"

"Tip offs to your private number and not to your official issue police mobile phone? Isn't that a little risky? And, I take it that Eddie McNerney is registered in the official register of informers then? Because I know he isn't, I have just checked. What's going on, Jez? I, like all the rest of the team respect you. You're one of the best DI's on the force to work for, you know that. Just what are you up to?" Sarah was taking a big gamble, but she didn't expect the response she got.

"What the hell then I'll tell you. You'll never make anything stick. I know how to cover my tracks as well as anyone, you won't be able to prove a thing. I'm just doing my little bit to reduce the crime rate, that's all. Nothing more; nothing less."

She looked at him, frowning, black eyebrows crooked in the furrow of her brow. "Are you telling me that you're involved in these killings?" said Sarah genuinely surprised.

"Involved? Involved? I'm not involved, Sarah, I've arranged each and every one. Every time we identify a gang leader, I make sure they are taken care of." Jez was becoming confident now, speaking calmly and eloquently. "Look, you know I'm a man of some considerable wealth, well together with a few like-minded individuals, we have decided to clean the scum bags of London off the streets; saving the taxpayers a fortune by the way. Do you know how many known felons are found not guilty when they eventually get to court?"

"Not exactly, no."

"Seventy three per cent, that's how many. Each of them hires a fancy lawyer who finds every loophole to get them off. As guilty as sin they are. Everyone knows it but they get off on some technicality or another after millions of pounds are spent on trials. So, we have decided to make the world a better place. A world where our grandchildren can grow up without the fear that is gripping today's society. The Tommy Sutcliffes of this world are scum and for a reasonable fee, paid to the right people, they can be," Jez paused a moment, "What shall I say? Disposed of, yes that's the best way of putting it. No body, no evidence, nothing. They just disappear, saving everyone a lot of bother. The best part is that no one even realises. They assume that they've gone to sunnier climes, to a beach somewhere to spend their ill-gotten gains. They are gone for ever."

"How many?" Sarah said.

"How many what? Oh, I don't know, four, five maybe. It'll be six pretty soon," said Jez, looking at his Breitling watch.

"Jez, you can't set yourself up as judge and jury."

"Judge, jury and executioner," corrected Jez. "That's us. The public would applaud us if they knew."

"But it's murder. Cold blooded murder, Jez. Our job is to stop that kind of thing, not perpetrate it. And what do you mean, 'six pretty soon?'"

"Nothing, Sarah, don't worry about it. Just press on with the Islington case and you'll do fine. You have a good career ahead of you, you know that don't you?" Jez said, making it clear that their conversation had come to an end.

Sarah sat opposite Jez, who was sitting there with his elbows on his desk looking as relaxed as if he was watching a test match at Lord's. She could hardly arrest her DCI. She didn't know what would happen to her next. Maybe she'd disappear under tons of concrete on a construction site somewhere in London.

"Okay. Well as you say, we'll never prove it," Sarah said as she stood up to leave the small office.

"Let me know how the Islington case progresses would you?" Jez said, looking back down at the papers on his desk.

Sarah slowly got up, opened the door and left Jez's offices, closing the door quietly behind her. She went to her desk and took out her mobile phone and with an almost indiscernible smile, she turned off the record mode.

Chapter Twelve

Sarah sat at her desk and leaned back in her chair, took a deep breath and tried to collect the thoughts that were spinning in her mind, out of control. She stared at the monitor in front of her. The screensaver was showing photographs of past holidays and past romances. She had no time for reminiscing. She needed a plan. Another murder was close and somehow she had to stop it.

"Is this yours?" Toby said, holding up a sheet of A4 paper with a grainy black and white photo on it.

"No, where did you find it?" Sarah said.

"It had slipped down the side of the printer. I saw you were printing something earlier and thought it was yours," replied Toby. "It must be Jez's then."

"Wait, let me take a look." Toby dropped the sheet of paper on Sarah's desk and returned to his work. Sarah picked up the paper and looked at the sinister face staring out at her, a man in his fifties, with close cropped hair, scar above his right eye. Why would Jez print this she wondered?

"Looks familiar," she said to no one in particular.

"What does?" Toby said, looking up from his monitor.

"This photo, any idea who it might be?" Sarah held up the sheet of paper so that Toby could see the face printed on it.

"No, I don't think so... wait a minute, isn't that Lewisham Larry?"

"Who?" Sarah said.

"Larry Tucker – otherwise known as Lewisham Larry. He ruled Southeast London a few years back. I haven't heard him mentioned for ages though."

Sarah was already busy typing the name of Larry Tucker into the CRO database. Lawrence Sebastian Tucker came onto her screen. The photo against his details was identical to the one printed on the sheet of paper that was in front of her. She quickly jotted down the address on to the sheet of paper which had the photograph printed on it. She shut down her computer, picked up her phone, grabbed her coat and made swiftly for the door.

"Where are you off to now?" Toby said.

"Just need to follow something up. Oh, and do me a favour, don't mention Lewisham Larry to Jez, or the photo you found will you?"

"Why would I?" Toby said, returning to his work.

Sarah walked along the bustling East London high street that ran past the front of the office. The colourful market stalls were doing a roaring trade. She was thinking through her next move when her mobile phone rang.

"Hello, Sarah Thompson."

"Sarah, it's Jane – I'm done with spas. I'm bored already, any news?"

"I was just about to ring you." Sarah turned through a small wrought iron gate into a neat garden area and sat on a green painted park bench.

Sarah brought Jane up to date with the events of the past half hour.

"So you think this Larry Tucker is target number six then do you?" Jane said.

"He has to be." Then, suddenly doubting herself, she added, "Doesn't he?"

"I guess so. Where do we find him?"

"I have his last known address from the CRO database. That seems as good a place to start as any. What did your controller say?"

"He's pulled me from the case. No debate, he lost someone last year from leaving them undercover too long and he won't make the same mistake twice. He thinks we're nearly there now anyway."

"So you're free to join forces with me now then?"

"Absolutely. Get your car, pick me up for the hotel and we'll pay Mr Tucker a visit."

"Will do, I'll be with you in ten minutes."

Sarah quickly got up from the bench and made her way back to the station.

*

"How long will it take us to get there?" Jane asked, as she buckled up her seat belt.

"Well, it's only seven miles but the traffic is solid at the moment so it could take hours. Blackwall Tunnel, North Greenwich on the A2 is the only sensible route. I know a few back doubles that should make it a bit quicker."

"Are you thinking what I'm thinking?" Jane said.

"What? That Larry could already be under two metres of concrete?"

"Exactly. The quicker the better I reckon."

Sarah didn't need asking a second time and she turned into a prohibited bus lane and accelerated past the stationary traffic to her right.

It was mid-afternoon before they slowly drove past the large steel faced gates. The gates were framed by two ornate pilasters, each one surmounted by a large stone dog with a paw raised as if warning visitors to stop and think again before entering.

"What do we do now? It doesn't exactly look welcoming does it?" Sarah said, staring at the vast gates in front of her.

"Watch and wait for a while I suggest, let's see if there are any comings or goings. It doesn't feel right, just barging in straight away."

"Agreed. Let's play it cool for a while. I'm starving; there's a newsagent at the end of the road. Fancy a sandwich?"

Sarah pulled into a 'residents' only' parking bay. This gave them a good view of the entrance to Larry Tucker's house. She got out of the car and left Jane watching while she went and bought some sandwiches.

*

Andy entered the site office and hurled his site helmet across his desk. He had just been summoned to see the school head and, as usual, she had done nothing to improve his mood.

"That woman is a pain in the arse."

"What does she want now?" Dave said.

"She only wants to move the toilets to the other side of the corridor."

"Well she can't," Dave said, "The under-slab drainage is installed and we'll have to break up half the ground floor slab to do that."

"Yes, Dave, thank you for telling me that. I did point that out to her ladyship but she is the head teacher and what she wants, she gets, apparently," Andy said.

"It'll delay the project by weeks."

"Not according to her it won't. But we'll use it our advantage. I'll have to talk to the architect and get someone down here sharpish. With Sylvie away skiing it'll mean we'll get someone who doesn't know the job which won't help at all. Oh, and I've sorted the order for the roof. Another loss against budget." Andy sighed as he sat at his desk.

"How much this time?" Dave said as he passed Andy a large white mug of strong coffee.

"About five grand. I'm not looking forward to Norman's visit here next week. He's not going to be happy. Apparently we priced for a cheaper option which was not specified. How could an estimator make such a basic mistake? No, don't answer that; a stupid question. Thanks for the coffee by the way."

"How's Jane?" Dave said, deciding to change the subject quickly. The question took Andy by surprise. He had already got himself back into his busy project and hadn't had a chance to properly think through the revelations of the past twenty four hours.

"She's fine. I saw her briefly last night."

"Things settling down a bit then are they?" Dave persisted.

"You could say that. I think I had better ring her, she's working far too hard at the moment."

Andy got up from his desk, went into the empty office opposite and dialled Jane's number. Having got her voicemail so many times recently, he was surprised when she answered.

"Hey, Andy, I wondered when you would call. Had a nice breakfast did you?"

"What? Oh yes, sorry about that. I thought I'd better get back to site, a lot going on at the moment."

"It's okay. I guessed. Are you okay? Any sign of trouble?" Jane said, sounding genuinely concerned.

"The only trouble I've got at the moment is with a megalomaniac head teacher and the delivery date for the roof."

"Well, you be careful. You should be alright; we have reason to believe that Eddie and his mates have other things on their minds at the moment."

"What do you mean? I thought Eddie would be behind bars by now. We saw the police taking him away from the house last night, or was that this morning?"

"He was released, Andy, without charge. Don't ask - it's complicated."

"Where are you now?" Andy said.

Jane brought him up to date with what Sarah had told her and explained where they were.

"You be careful. Have you got back up?" he said.

Jane laughed and said, "We're somewhat on our own on this one at the moment."

"I'm planning on going home tonight. I'm shattered and need my own bed. That'll be okay, won't it?"

"Yes, should be, keep your eyes open for anything unusual but I think you'll be safe there," Jane said.

"Will you be home tonight?" Andy added, almost as an afterthought.

"Who knows? I'd like to be, I still have a lot of explaining to do. I'll let you know, take care. 'Bye."

Andy disconnected the call, put his phone back into his pocket and returned to his office.

"You actually managed to speak to her then? That makes a change," Dave said.

"Yes, she's okay," replied Andy.

"Another exciting day in the world of forensic accounting is it?" Dave said sarcastically.

"You could say that. Have you completed today's labour sheets?"

"Not yet," said Dave.

"Well I suggest you get on with them, I'm not staying late tonight that's for sure."

It was just after four o'clock when Andy left the office. Dave agreed to lock up when the last of the bricklayers had finished for the day.

Andy headed off in the direction of Canning Town underground station and as he turned the first corner he was confronted by a line of blue and white police tape across the road and pavement. He looked up and saw several police vans and cars, blue lights flashing and a large group of police outside one of the houses further down the street. His first feeling was one of fear, they had caught up with him at last; but then he realised that the focus of their attention was elsewhere. Another drugs raid, Andy thought. He had already witnessed several during his time working in the area. He went up to the tape cautiously to see if he would be allowed through and was met by a young police officer complete with body armour.

"Sorry sir, you can't come through here."

"What's going on?"

"Sorry sir, I can't tell you that. You'll have to find another route home."

Andy turned around without saying another word and headed in the direction of the steak house where he and Steve had eaten the previous evening. The diversion also took him down Shackleton Road, the scene of last night's escapade. He really didn't want to go along that road again but didn't have any choice.

He walked on the opposite side of the road from house number seventy two and was surprised to see the recognisable GON registration of the white Ford Transit van.

The Concrete Grave

Surely the police would've impounded it, he thought. This time it was parked on the opposite side of the road to the house. So Andy walked past it. As he drew level with the van he thought he heard something, a low but audible groan. He stopped, listened, but heard nothing so he continued walking. Andy had no intention of hanging around in an area that he wouldn't exactly be welcomed. As he drew level with the front of the van he heard the noise again, this time it was slightly louder and accompanied by the sound of scuffing. Someone or something was definitely in the van.

Andy took a few paces back until he was level with the body of the van. "Hello, anyone there?" he said as quietly as he could.

The reply came in a series of loud and more regular grunts with a louder banging as if someone was stamping on the floor of the van.

Possibly due to the goings on over the last two days, Andy immediately pictured someone bound and gagged inside the van. He wasn't sure what to do; almost without thinking he tried the rear door handles which were not only locked but supplemented by a solid looking hasp and staple, secured by a large padlock. Clearly someone wanted to protect the contents of their van. Andy walked to the front of the van ensuring that the he kept it between himself and the house opposite. He looked through the side window but the rear section had been closed off from behind the front seats.

He had to do something, but he wasn't sure what, so he walked on and for the second night running went into The Carpenter's Arms to gain some thinking time.

The Concrete Grave

On entering he immediately looked across to the table where his friend from the night before had sat. Sure enough, there he was again. Andy had no intention of going anywhere near him this time so he made for the opposite end of the bar where he ordered half a pint of lager. It was not yet six o'clock and the pub was much quieter and a lot less threatening than it had been the previous night.

He sat at an empty table in the corner, took out his phone and rang Jane. He still hadn't properly got his head around her actual occupation but, thinking about it, she was the obvious person to talk to at this time.

"Hi, Andy," Jane answered cheerily.

"Hi, how are you getting on?" Andy said.

"Nothing here, we just tried to gain access by the intercom but it appears that no one is home." Andy told Jane about his walk to the underground station, his finding the white Ford Transit van and his suspicions regarding the contents. Before he'd finished explaining the full situation Jane had taken the phone from her ear, covered the mouthpiece and said, "Andy's found him - head for Shackleton Road – now."

"Jane? Jane? Are you still there?" Andy said.

Sarah started the car and, with a squeal of tyres, headed north towards the River Thames.

"Yes, I'm still here. Where are you exactly right now?"

"I'm in the Carpenter's Arms just up the road from the house."

"Stay there, Andy, and don't move, we're on our way, but it is rush hour now, so we will be a while. Just sit tight and do nothing until we get there."

The penny had dropped and Andy said, "You don't think it's Sydenham Sid in that van do you?"

"Lewisham Larry," Jane corrected, "Yes, it's highly possible, and if you heard sounds it means he's not yet dead."

"I'll move to a position where I can keep an eye on the van then."

"Okay, but don't do anything. If you see anything suspicious call me a once."

"Will do," Andy said as he put the phone back in his pocket.

He moved to a table that looked through the leaded glass windows. It was almost dark now but he could still see the white van under the street lights.

Andy tried to estimate the time the girls would take to travel from Lewisham to Tower Hamlets; he guessed it would be at least an hour, so he got another pint and maintained his watch on the street.

Just before seven o'clock Andy was getting bored; his mind was wandering, so much had happened in the past two weeks that he wasn't sure what was reality and what wasn't. Just as he was considering a third pint he saw some movement from the house opposite the van. Two men, one looking very much like Eddie, were purposefully crossing the road towards the van. Andy quickly got up and left the pub. There was no way he could let them get away and he was the only person who could stop them.

As he walked along the dark street he quickly phoned Jane and told her what was happening.

"Stay exactly where you are, Andy, we're not far now, don't do anything rash," Jane said.

"Okay," said Andy as he hung up.

He walked along the pavement, keeping as close to the hedge on his right as he could. He saw one of the men open the rear doors of the van. He was now within twenty metres and they hadn't seen him.

He heard a volley of violent swearing, followed by, "He's not dead!"

He then heard the other voice say, "You're kidding – he took two to the heart I'm sure of it."

"Well, he's moaning and groaning still."

"Get out of the way. Let me finish the job properly."

Andy could see that the man he initially thought to be Eddie, very definitely was Eddie. Andy reacted instinctively; he suddenly pushed the other man aside and into the hedge. Eddie reached inside his jacket and, even in the dim light, Andy could clearly see that he was now holding a gun which was pointed into the back of the van with the sole intention of finishing the job they had originally intended.

Without thinking Andy ran straight at Eddie with the new found confidence he had discovered over the past twenty four hours, and hit him full force with his right shoulder before he could fire. The force of the collision was such that both men fell into a heap in the centre of the road. Andy found himself on top and started pummelling Eddie with punches. Unfortunately for Andy none of them had much effect. The East End gangster was strong, very strong. He pushed up hard and sent Andy flying backwards.

"What the hell do you think you're doing?" Eddie cursed. Then slowly he recognised who his assailant was, hardly believing what he was seeing.

"Andy Walker!" He mixed in a few expletives and now Eddie was mad. "I've had just about as much of you as I can stand. I should have finished you off last night, I'm not going to make the same mistake again."

He pointed his pistol, which he had managed to keep a grip of, at Andy's chest. He took a couple of paces back as if to get a proper aim. Andy quickly got his feet and turned to run, he heard a sudden crack, like the branch of the tree snapping and felt a violent pain across his chest. His legs buckled and he felt himself falling into a heap.

Andy tried to look up to see what was going on, trying to blink quickly to bring his fading world back into focus but he couldn't. His eyelids were suddenly too heavy. Loss of blood? He put his right hand inside his coat and felt his chest in the area where the initial pain was; his chest was wet and warm.

He heard a noise, a faint and distant noise. It sounded like car tyres screeching. The pain was excruciating, he had to keep conscious, he knew that. But he was losing his battle, he was aware of blackness, a terrible pain, then nothing.

Chapter Thirteen

Andy saw a clean white light. It was coming to him through a bright shining tunnel. He had read about this, seen television programmes. Was this it? The end of the road?

His mouth felt dry. He wanted a drink. His head ached and it felt disconnected from the rest of his body. He heard distant voices. Was this heaven, he wondered? Or maybe the other place. What happens next?

"Andy? Andy? Can you hear me?"

Andy recognised the voice but couldn't quite place it. It took too much effort to try. He tried to move his mouth. He was aware of nothing but a shallow groan being emitted from it. He then felt himself drifting, floating almost.

"Andy, it's Jane. Are you awake?"

"Yes, I think so," Andy forced himself to say. "Where am I?"

"You're in hospital. You're in very good hands. You're going to be okay."

"What happened?"

"You received a nasty bullet wound to the chest," an authoritative voice said. "I'm Nurse Fielder, and my job is to get you better, the less you speak at the moment the better."

"Jane?" Andy murmured.

"I'm here, Andy. I've been beside you all along. Get some sleep and we'll talk when you are ready."

*

It was a further two days before Andy was well enough to hold a sensible conversation. He was propped up in bed on three pillows. He had tubes going everywhere and he could now see Jane and Sarah sitting to the right of his bed.

"Is someone going to tell me what happened?" Andy said, somewhat testily.

"You were shot, Andy. The bullet missed your heart by less than a centimetre and you lost a lot of blood," Jane said.

"How long have I been here?"

"Almost a week. You have been very ill, Andy. We've all been extremely worried."

"A week? Well I suppose that explains the headache. Who shot me?"

"Eddie McNerney. Sarah and I arrived as the shot was fired. When I received your call I phoned for backup and an armed response unit turned up moments after us. Eddie and his henchmen surrendered without a fight. Eddie's gang are safely behind bars, as is Jez Lloyd-Brown. My recording of Jez's confession was more than enough to bring him down." Sarah said, taking over from Jane. "A sad end for a good police officer who decided to take justice into his own hands."

"Was he working alone?" Andy asked.

"No, we don't believe so. We think that he was backed by some of his well-heeled Cambridge chums. But Jez refuses to reveal anything, so I doubt if we'll ever find out who they are."

"What about the body in the van?" Andy said, as that fateful evening started slowly coming back to him.

"You saved his life. It was indeed Larry Tucker. He had been shot and left for dead, but was in fact still alive. He'd lost a lot of blood, but he'll pull through. He's just down the corridor from here actually, surrounded by armed police."

"And what about me?"

"What do you mean? You'll pull through okay."

"No, I didn't mean that. I have been instrumental in burying a human being under ten cubic metres of concrete. Will I go inside?"

"No, not at all," Jane said laughing. "You were working with us on the case. It was all part of the plan to bring to justice a gang of very evil men and a corrupt police officer. I've told the Chief Constable that you are willing to testify and he has agreed not to press charges."

"And the ten thousand pounds?"

"Hmmm, I'd forgotten about that. That'll have to be surrendered to the authorities. I hope you haven't spent it all."

"No, not much of it."

"In any case, I've already had a couple of calls from the national papers wanting your story, so I guess you'll make more from that."

"Then we should have enough for an end of case celebration meal at *The Ivy*." Sarah smiled.

"Sounds like a deal," Jane replied.

"So, that's it, it's all over at last then," Andy said.

"Not quite," said Jane, "There's someone here to see you."

Jane stood up and opened the door. Dave walked in holding a half-eaten bunch of grapes.

"Hello, Andy. We've got a problem with those bloody scaffolders!"

ACKNOWLEDGEMENTS

This book would not have been completed without the support of many friends and family. My grateful thanks go to everyone who has contributed in some way to the final product.

Special thanks go to my editing and proof reading team of Emma Tait, Philip Chown and Gill Gloster. My daughter Emma for her forthright comments, Philip for not allowing me to 'overstretch the elastic band of credibility' and Gill for her forensic eye for detail. Not forgetting Helen O'Connell for her early input and advice.

Many thanks to the various people who provided technical support: Stuart Rawlings for information on money laundering, and Emma Tait and Mark Newton for their medical advice.

Also thanks to Ben Deavin, my son, for his cover design.

I am also grateful to Janet, my long suffering wife, who thought I was mad to undertake this project, but who humoured me and answered my many questions about word choice, punctuation and typing.

Finally to all the friends I have made whilst working in the construction industry; many of you have contributed in some small way to this book – even if you didn't know it.

ABOUT THE AUTHOR

Mike Deavin grew up in Essex, England and has worked for over forty years in the construction industry. He spent several years as a director of a main contractor based on the south coast of England and is now working as a freelance consultant. The Concrete Grave is his first book. He lives in Surrey with his wife Janet.

Printed in Great Britain
by Amazon.co.uk, Ltd.,
Marston Gate.